CURTAIN FALL

By Eileen Dewhurst

CURTAIN FALL
TRIO IN THREE FLATS
DRINK THIS
DEATH CAME SMILING
AFTER THE BALL

CURTAIN FALL

EILEEN DEWHURST

PUBLISHED FOR THE CRIME CLUB BY
DOUBLEDAY & COMPANY, INC.
GARDEN CITY, NEW YORK
1982

To my Mother

All of the characters in this book are fictitious, and any resemblance to actual persons, living or dead, is purely coincidental.

ISBN: 0-385-18184-1
Library of Congress Catalog Card Number 82-45071

Printed in the United States of America
First Edition in the United States

CHAPTER 1

I

On a sunny August morning Joanna Stuart said to herself without warning, yet without surprise:

"I can't cope."

She had just completed a series of telephone calls fielding a team of drivers for the old ladies' monthly tea party and she was still sitting in the hall, on the upright chair beside the telephone.

Joanna formed the words with her lips, staring ahead of her at the white front door with its little wooden panes of window, but seeing a swirling abstract which even as she watched it moved faster and faster.

"I—can't—cope."

It wasn't the usual exaggeration which she had used, and heard used, a hundred times and more during the course of her good works, it was a solemn statement of fact.

It was also a revelation, in the sense that yesterday—even two minutes ago—she had had no inkling of it.

But it hadn't really come out of the blue, it was the culmination of a process which had been going on for a long time. For a long time there had been a scream deep down inside her which was getting closer and closer to her throat and which when it broke surface would ring out all over the district and everyone would know what she really was.

"What am I, really?" she always asked herself, as she felt the scream rising, searching the memories which ran along as constant accompaniment to her extrovert days, of a time when she and Peter and their home had been the centre of her life and she and Peter had done things solely to please themselves. As she presided over her committees and chatted up her old ladies, it was as if a home movie was being screened in a quiet part of her mind, showing herself and Peter as they had once been, in house and garden, driving about the countryside and the coast.

It wasn't that these pictures reminded Joanna of a *happier* time than the time where she now found herself (and anyway the word *happy* was not relevant to her life either then or now), it was just that they were so different, and they made her wonder vaguely how and why things had changed . . .

She was still sitting on the upright chair when the telephone rang. She picked it up at once.

"Joanna Stuart."

"Oh, Mrs. Stuart, forgive me, it's Nancy Edwards . . ."

"Yes, Nancy?"

"We're having a bit of trouble getting our complement for the mongol children group this morning . . . Mrs. Mathers had to go to her sister . . ."

"Have you tried Mrs. James?"

"Yes. I've tried everybody, Mrs. Stuart."

Joanna didn't hesitate.

"All right, Nancy, I'll come myself. Not to worry."

"Oh, thank you, Mrs. Stuart."

"That's all right. I'll be there by eleven." Now she paused. "It's getting to be a shambles, isn't it? Can you stay on a few minutes after the children have gone and we'll try to work out a fresh rota?"

"Yes, of course."

Joanna put the receiver down, wondering why she was envying Nancy Edwards, and then deciding it was because of the probability that Nancy knew who she was, or else never considered the question. The order and clarity of mind which while she was busy kept the scream well in check disintegrated, and she said with more certainty than the first time, and aloud:

"I can't cope."

She recognised a faint sense of relief. She didn't, any longer, want to cope. She wanted to belong to herself again, although not in the old way, not in the way of the early years of her marriage.

Joanna looked round the hall in bewilderment. What was she doing there? She felt for a sharp second as if she had no past at all, as if she had been born into that moment in the hall, born on to the chair beside the telephone, naked into the world except for a few disturbing memories of a previous existence. The only thing she felt certain of was that, at the age of thirty-seven, she had not yet lived in the way she should. Her certainty of this was like the great tree she had once come upon while walking—when? where? had she been alone?—looming out of a thick white ground mist.

Good works were not Joanna Stuart, although it appeared she did them well. The exclusivity of her early marriage was not.

And now there was only one course left. She could no longer cope.

2

Had it—whatever it was—begun with her miscarriage? Daphne, who was her wisest friend, had said one should try and divert oneself in every possible way when one was trying to outlive a tragedy, above all by helping other less fortunate people. Tragedy . . . Daphne had used a strong word. But she must have listened to Daphne. She must have started to be frantically busy after the specialist had told her she could never have a baby.

She wasn't sure. She couldn't remember. All she knew was the present where she found herself, and the old movie that kept running of her and Peter in the early days. Perhaps the trouble was that Peter was away so much. Joanna shifted uneasily on the telephone chair.

At one time she and Peter had been too self-absorbed, she accepted that, but there was a happy mean, and now she didn't belong to herself at all. She had over-corrected, and all at once it was intolerable . . .

Joanna got up off the chair and went and did a few things about the house and started the sprinkler going on the brown lawn and had a coffee at the kitchen table. She hardly noticed what she was doing because she had begun to have practical thoughts about the Window.

She had seen the Window only once, only for a very few moments, and a long time ago. She and Peter had been driving through a small seaside town on a forlorn autumn evening when the grey sea had seemed too bleak, and she had turned away from it and looked straight at the first floor bay window of a small white stuccoed hotel.

She had just had time to note that the hotel bore in dull gold lettering the honest title of *Seaview* and then they had gone past. She wasn't sure at the time what had happened, although she knew that something had, but soon afterwards she discovered that the Window and the hotel in which it was set and the strange sensation of intensity and regret which had come to her from the grey sea had passed intact into the background of her mind, to be called up countless times for re-experience. She had never shared the experience with Peter, and she knew as time went on that the fact of keeping it to herself meant she was keeping more and more from him.

The hotel and the Window she could always see with sharp physical clarity: white stucco a bit dingy and flaking in patches, yellow paint round the frames of the floor-length sashed panes and round the larger bay windows to each side of the front door. More and more she had come to see herself behind the first floor Window as some sort of important, if vague and distant, goal. At times it was almost as if the real part of her was already there, waiting to welcome and re-unite with the part that had just been talking to Nancy Edwards. The Window had in fact become a symbol of her essential self.

At a quarter to eleven Joanna went out to the car. She could no longer cope, but she could cope for the length of the morning in her knowledge of this, and because she knew there was something she could do to prevent the scream finding its way to the surface.

3

Mongol children are without any instinct of self-aggrandisement, they have no wish to go one better than the next child. Their contentment resides entirely in themselves and in smiling faces round them, and so while they will weep and rage at the loss of something they have been enjoying (as when Joanna turned down the volume of the transistor radio: they are musical), their play is without reference to their neighbour and they are less mentally harassing to oversee in quantities than normal children—although they can more easily get themselves into physical trouble.

Joanna loved them and never found them sad. Today as always

she gave all her attention to each child in turn, cuddling the smallest and receiving delighted response (mongol children have no sadistic impulses, they never attempt to hurt by withholding evidence of the pleasure you give them), and had no thoughts beyond the room where she now found herself. When the children had all been collected or taken home she sat down with Nancy Edwards and the other two helpers and with the aid of the telephone devised a rota for the next three months which took care of the possibility of undermanning.

She would have done this even if she had not discovered that she could no longer cope.

Driving home she turned her head once or twice towards the houses that lined the road, imagining how it would be when she saw the Window again. When she let herself into the empty house she stopped in the hall and looked at herself curiously in the long mirror. She had been slim and now she was thin, but still looked younger than she was. With her short almost straight brown hair from a little distance, in a poor light, she could have been a young girl. It surprised her, somehow, that there was no expression on her face, beyond vague inquiry. She thought of pretending a smile to see what it looked like, but instead turned away. She went upstairs and got a suitcase out and filled it with summer clothes. She rang up the milkman and the newsagent and the laundry and her daily woman's sister-in-law with a message. She shied away from ringing Daphne. She had a cup of coffee and some toast.

Then she went into the garden and turned off the sprinkler, and left a note in the greenhouse for the old man who came twice a week to help them keep the garden tidy. She stood for a few moments experiencing a pang of anxiety for her garden without her. It was the only feeling she remembered experiencing for what seemed a very long time. She looked round her in a sort of dull surprise.

"What am I, really?

"I am not the present. Nor the past."

Eventually she shrugged and went back into the house and turned off the water. It was while she was in the contorted position necessary to reach the key that the strangest feeling of muddle came over her. She couldn't remember whether Peter was in Brussels or Amsterdam, nor the day on which he was due to come home. When she tried to concentrate and think she felt so dizzy she had to sit down and stick her head between her knees, so she gave it up.

Finally she went through the house locking doors and seeing that all heat and light was turned off, put her suitcase into the car, and left.

CHAPTER 2

I

As soon as she was in the car and driving towards the Window, Joanna no longer felt in a hurry. She stopped after about an hour to consult the map and when she was sure of the rest of the way to Linton-on-Sea she opened the window wide, lit a cigarette and leaned back in her seat.

The smoke curled slowly, white against the blue sky. The place where she had pulled in was not particularly beautiful, a lay-by beside a dual carriageway with traffic roaring regularly past, but to Joanna at that moment the immediate world was dazzling because it had become real. The spindly sycamores which lined the lay-by, the cigarette packet and lolly stick and paper bags which had overflowed the litter bins or been thrown wide of them, the warm sun on her face, these were real. The light seemed very bright, even through her sunglasses. The only thought she had to be wary of was Peter, and for the moment it was too insubstantial to disturb her new excitement. She couldn't remember when she had last looked forward to something.

"It is better to travel than to arrive."

She mouthed these words too, just under her breath. Someone well known had said them first. Were they true? Certainly, this part of her pilgrimage, at least, she was sure of. As she manoeuvred back on to the road Joanna's excitement was shot through with apprehension . . .

She had crossed the county border now and had reached a part of the country which was unfamiliar. In one stretch of old suburb demolition was under way. Half the compact Victorian villa still stood, and the remaining front window reminded Joanna of the Window . . . She pulled sharply in to the pavement, switched off the engine, and sat with her forehead resting on the edge of the steering-wheel and her eyes tightly closed.

Fool. Fool. Fool. Because her memories had turned out to be immortal, that didn't mean the subject of them must be immortal too. The only thing from that far-off mystical encounter that she could be sure of seeing again was the sea, and even that would be a different colour, it would be blue. And across the road from it there could be a space, or another building.

Joanna started the engine and moved blindly away from the pavement. It was as well that the car she almost ran into hooted so loudly, because she stopped then, shocked, and waited until she had pulled herself together.

Now, when she went on, she saw only signposts. She drove without stopping, although she grew thirsty and her back was damp against the vinyl seat. Her realisation of the fragility of her lifeline had been brutal but eventually, slowly, there re-entered her spirit the relief of freedom and decision, and that was better than quenching her thirst. By the time she saw the sea she had recovered enough to recognise that the new future would still be awaiting her even if its symbol was not.

2

The sea was pale blue like the sky. The air was cooler at last, and she smelled salt. The tide was a little out and the strip of sand gleamed apricot. *Seaview* was—had been—to the west of Linton, and she would come on it—or on where it had been—before she reached the town. She drove along beside bare grassy dunes, and a notice of the intended erection of flats made her heart thump. At last the buildings began: a few small privately-owned houses; a block of larger houses with notices in their windows announcing holiday accommodation, deck chairs in the small front gardens, optimistically meteorological names set into the glass of the porches, like *Sunny Bank* and *Fair Winds*—these weren't new, at any rate; a small cinema from the heyday of cinema building (all its cinema announcements obliterated but at least standing); another block, and then she was level with the front of it and it was called *Seaview* in dull gold lettering and immediately above the lettering was the Window.

The lay-by outside the hotel was full of cars, and Joanna veered across the road to the low sea wall, stopped the car, and sat still, looking out over the sea towards a horizon lost in the haze of settled weather, marked only by the pale shadow of a ship. Then she turned towards the hotel. The paint round the windows was still yellow, the stucco was still white but now without blemish, there were three men in dark city suits coming down the path from the front door and a strikingly pretty girl lounging in a long chair on the small front lawn who raised her head to look curiously after them.

One of the men looked across at Joanna as he opened the door of a large car in the lay-by. He said something to his companions and they looked at her too, with the sort of lingering look the girl in the lounging chair had just given them, and then they all got into the car and drove away towards Linton.

Joanna started her engine again, and slid across the road into the space the men had left. She found her handbag and cardigan and got out of the car, then for the first time stood in front of her grail.

She wanted to stand there indefinitely, just looking up at the Window and back at the sea and at the Window again, breathing the soft salt air, but the girl was now staring at her with such open avid curiosity that she felt forced to walk up the path and in at the front door.

The square hall was furnished comfortably and with taste, and there was a series of watercolour maritime views on the pale walls. There was no one to be seen, either in the hall or in the office behind the polished wooden counter that announced itself as Reception. Joanna saw a typewriter with paper in it and heard a distant indignant female voice. There was a brass bell on the counter and she moved across the hall, slowly, and eventually pressed it. The sharp sound brought a youngish woman moving quickly from a part of the office which was out of sight of the hall. She was subdued in every way—skin, hair, clothes—and Joanna didn't think it was her voice that she had just heard. The woman said pleasantly, but pushing her hair back from her forehead in a tired gesture:

"Can I help you?"

Now that the vital moment had come Joanna found it difficult to speak, despite the woman's small encouraging smile, her lips were stiff. But eventually she faltered out, feeling childish:

"I should–like to stay here."

She thought the woman was surprised. She thought the surprise was followed by a look of suspicion. But it couldn't be, and she could hardly believe she was listening to the woman's next words.

"I'm afraid I must ask if you're a reporter. If you are . . . I'm sorry . . ."

"A–reporter? I don't understand . . ."

Only a fine actress could have feigned Joanna's crestfallen response. The woman's face partly cleared.

"Forgive me. But you'll appreciate . . ."

For a mad moment Joanna imagined herself in some realm where one had to justify fulfilment of one's heart's desire. She found herself explaining.

"It was years ago. I passed your hotel–and I liked the look of it. I promised myself that one day . . . Then I suddenly got a chance to come away, and I just came . . . It was that big front window . . ."

There was, again, a strange look in the woman's eyes. She asked Joanna to excuse her for a moment and disappeared into the recesses of the office. While Joanna was waiting another man in a dark city suit came into the hall through a door at the back, looked at her, then stood negligently beside a notice board crammed with leaflets informing of the current attractions of Linton-on-Sea. When the woman returned she was accompanied by another: older and fatter and with elaborately piled blue-grey hair, a lot of make-up in the midst of which she sported a large sprouting mole as if it was a beauty spot, and an air of authority.

"I understand you are asking for a room." This was the voice which had so recently been angry.

"Yes!" Joanna heard her injured tone, and would have been amused if she had not felt so puzzled and anxious. "I passed your hotel some time ago, I liked the look of it, I was suddenly free to come away and I just lit out and came . . ."

Only then did she realise that a natural alternative to coming would have been to telephone, but she had never thought of it–no doubt because she had wanted to be sure of travelling hopefully.

The women looked at one another, Joanna wondered if the older woman had looked towards the man who was still standing by the notice board, and then she felt dizzy and had to lean her arm on the counter and her head on her hand. She thought she heard the man say, wearily:

"Not another one! All right, all right, business as usual," and then the younger of the two women in the office was handing her a glass of water. After drinking some she felt better.

"I'm sorry . . ."

"That's quite all right!"

The older woman elbowed the younger out of the way. She opened a book which was lying on the counter. "You're fortunate. We have just one vacant room, and I understand it is the room for which you expressed a particular wish." She turned the book round to face Joanna. "Will you please sign the register?"

3

Joanna went straight over to the Window and stood there with her hand on the frame. Without turning round she thanked the girl who had preceded her up the stairs with her suitcase and she went on standing there after she heard the door close. The Window did reach to the ground, and inside the room the frames were painted white. An upper sash was open and she could hear voices from the garden and still smell the sea. To her left the promenade curved out of sight into the centre of the town, and across the colourless glitter of the water she saw the far end of the curve, and of the town, a white line of buildings against a green hill.

She breathed a long sigh of relief.

The voices in the garden below were growing louder and more excited. There was a theatrical-sounding peal of laughter. Joanna looked down and saw that a redheaded girl had joined the honey blonde, perching on the foot of the lounging chair. When she concentrated Joanna could hear what they were saying.

"Seems—kind of weird, doesn't it?"

"D'you mean her? Or everything?"

"Everything, really."

"Yeah."

Each girl was brightly and scantily clad, each had a perfect long slim body, each a sort of brilliance which left Joanna with an idea, despite the slightly demotic English voices, of something foreign.

Suddenly, as if activated by a single mind, the girls looked up at the Window, straight into Joanna's gaze. She overcame her impulse to step hastily out of sight and made herself move backwards slowly and with a deprecating smile, which was not acknowledged in the dual steady stare. The expression in the eyes was indefinable, although the thought *fear* flashed into Joanna's mind and was incredulously dismissed. She remained just out of sight of the Window, waiting shamelessly to eavesdrop again.

There was a short silence followed by muffled laughter, hysteria-edged.

"Anyway, what's this latest instalment, for goodness' sake?"

"Instalment—that's good."

"I didn't mean to make a pun, cleverclogs."

"No, you're just naturally brilliant."

There was the sort of giggle a girl makes when she half fears, half hopes, that somebody is going to push her into the water.

"No, honestly, though, Rhoda—d'you think it's got anything to do with . . ."

The voice had sunk, sobered. Like the answering voice.

"Perhaps it's one of the family."

"They'd hardly put her in *there*. I think it's just a nutter . . ."

"*Sh!*"

The dialogue broke down in laughter. There was the sound of sandals slapping on to stone. Joanna stood bewildered and dismayed, and then she remembered that she had reached the room behind the Window. She had travelled and arrived. Nothing else in the world counted beside that, and she turned to survey her treasure.

CHAPTER 3

I

It was a big room, square except for the facets of the Window. Sunlight streamed in, and over years of summers it had faded the gold of mahogany and carpet and upholstery. The shabby armchair was drawn up beside a fireplace with a white surround symmetrically embossed with the trailing tendrils of *art nouveau* flowers. The room was clinically clean.

Joanna unpacked slowly and carefully, enjoying the process as much as she remembered ever enjoying anything before. There was far more space than she needed and when she had put all her clothes neatly away she struggled her suitcase up on top of the enormous wardrobe (it had *art nouveau* floral panels set into the mahogany on each side of the long mirror) and sat down in the armchair.

Now when she turned to the Window she could see only the serene pale blue of the sky. At first she could hear voices in the garden and it seemed to her that all of them, whatever the accent or lack of it, had an articulation and a resonance which made them larger than voices usually were, that every laugh was the *fortissimo* essence of laughter, every mock scream of dismay a perfect example of that social device. She thought it was because she had wakened up to her surroundings after a long coma. It surprised her mildly that she didn't get out of the armchair and go and look, but there was plenty of time. She hadn't known how tired she was.

Eventually the voices ceased, and then she heard them again on the landing. A little later—a few minutes? an hour?—a low reverberation sounded up the stairs.

Joanna jumped to her feet. Dinner! Abruptly she remembered the curious reactions of the two women in the office. But she was now living behind the Window and she went downstairs eager to meet whatever the hotel had to offer her and, above all, the owners of the disembodied voices.

But the hall was empty and when she went into the dining-room there was no one there except for the women from the office, sharing a table for two. They nodded coolly to Joanna as she was led by the girl over to another small table, against the wall, and when they had finished their meal they left without looking at her again.

Here was another mystery. And a disappointment. What had become of the owners of all those animated voices, of the hands that had slammed bedroom and bathroom doors, the feet she had heard on the stairs?

Joanna was so preoccupied she had almost finished her meal before she realised how good it was. And the mystery was intensified by the fact that the tables were laid for breakfast, and there were used napkins in rings . . .

Sauce bottles clustered on a side table made her remember going into the dining-room of a small hotel a long time ago, to have lunch with an aunt who lived there and from whom her mother thought there were expectations. In that hotel, the population of the dining-room had been seated, with the exception of her aunt and herself, one apiece at identical small tables. There had been something infinitely depressing about the quiet room with its rows of evenly spaced little kingdoms, sad or suspicious-eyed men and women (predominantly women) each presiding over his or her own small round of cutlery, glass, crockery and sauce bottles . . . It could only have been the sauce bottles which had brought up the memory, *Seaview* was entirely different, with its bay window overlooking the sea and haphazard arrangement of tables.

"Would you like coffee here, madam, or in the lounge?"

Joanna looked at the girl, who was young and untidy. She had a gentle face which Joanna thought she might be trying to make severe. When Joanna asked her her name she said "Margaret" curtly.

"I'll have coffee in the lounge, Margaret." Perhaps she would find someone in the lounge.

But the lounge was deserted too, although there was a library book with a Linton bookplate and a bookmark on a side table and a couple of well-handled newspapers. Sipping the coffee which Margaret quickly brought her, Joanna decided that the mystery was pleasurable rather than not, and that solitude at *Seaview* was something to be savoured. She could only be imagining a hostility in these strangers, she knew her reactions had become unpredictable.

The lounge matched the dining-room and its window formed the twin bay. The promenade was also deserted. The sun had set, but as she looked out pink spread and deepened in the sky, lipped up and over each small ridge of water. She would have a short walk and then she would go to bed.

"Mind if I join you?"

Joanna was so deeply, so almost somnolently, resigned to the prospect of no further human contact that day, she gave a little shriek. The man froze for a just noticeable second, half-way to sitting down in the armchair opposite, looking at her keenly. It was the man she had seen on her arrival, studying the notice board in the hall. Seeing him for a second time Joanna realised that she had already received from him a vague sensation of alarm. Not that there was anything menacing in his appearance or manner, despite those alert eyes. Perhaps it was that they didn't quite accord with his lazy smile and relaxed posture in the chair (she already thought she could have imagined the reflex stiffening of a moment earlier). In fact he was so relaxed, a total stranger, she felt he was only just avoiding insolence. Her usual reaction, in the latest phase of her life at least, would have been a breezy formality. But it seemed that she had changed and all she could summon up was a mild curiosity with, somewhere behind it, a waiting irritation should the peace of her evening be threatened.

Joanna realised, not without a throb of pleasure, that the woman who had arrived at *Seaview* was inclined to be selfish.

"You *have* joined me, it seems."

The man made a little bow of acknowledgement. Margaret arrived and put coffee in front of him. Her manner to him was as curt as it had been to Joanna.

"Hold on, Margaret love"—the girl remained impassive under the verbal familiarity—"I'll have a brandy. For you . . . ?" He gestured towards Joanna.

"No, thank you."

"So be it, Margaret. One brandy. The usual."

Margaret perhaps sniffed. She went away and Joanna looked at the man as he poured his coffee. About thirty, rather nattily suited, undeniably good-looking in any canon—dark, wavy-haired, long-lashed, with small strong features. His canine teeth were slightly pointed, giving him a predatory air which the watchful eyes did nothing to contradict. Joanna thought he was over average height, and lean. He said to her:

"So you wanted the front room."

The statement made her feel defensive. "Yes!"

"You were lucky to get it. The hotel's full."

"Full?"

"Except for your room."

"But—there's no one here! Nobody for dinner! Yet there were people . . . two girls . . . voices . . . In the garden and upstairs. But no one but me had dinner!"

All at once the mystery was excruciating. Joanna watched him eagerly for a clue, and was surprised to see amazement and disbelief cross his face. He said:

"You don't know any of the guests, then?"

"Any of which guests? No, you're right, I don't!"

"I see."

"*I* don't!"

But he sat back in his chair, drinking coffee. Joanna felt vaguely uneasy. For the second time since her arrival, she had the crazy feeling that perhaps she had travelled in the spirit rather than the flesh, as if the rules of nature were suspending.

Yet she found, again, that it was more exhilarating than disturbing. The only discordant feeling that still hovered was irritability. She said coldly:

"You have come to some important conclusion?"

The man leaned forward, so swiftly Joanna drew back.

"I think I may have done. What made you come to *Seaview?*"

She opened her mouth for a freezing response but the man was smiling so easily and amiably, and it seemed so unimportant to stand on her dignity, she found herself telling him. Perhaps too she welcomed an opportunity to talk about her coming to *Seaview,* it was so much more important to her than anything else.

Not that it was easy to explain why she had come.

"I felt—choked. Too much to do. I'd got—out of touch with myself."

"So you decided on *Seaview* because you'd been so happy here in the past."

"No."

"No?"

"I was never here in the past. Except—in my imagination."

"Castle in Spain?" The man's eyebrows rose. Occasionally there was an openness of vowel which made her think he came from London. "*Seaview* is an unlikely candidate."

"Nevertheless," said Joanna firmly. "Look, I was driving through Linton with my husband once and passed the hotel and it just sort of—stuck in my head. Don't ask me why. When I decided—I had to come away, I thought of it. And I came."

"Where from?"

She told him, without comment on his nosiness, where she lived.

"And you came all that way, in the summer, without telephoning first, without attempting to book a room?"

Now she must start to be wary. No one must know the importance of the Window in her life for so long, because they would think she was mad, and anyway no one would be able to understand it. She herself accepted it with faith rather than understanding.

"It was a gesture," she said. "I was suddenly at the end of my tether, and I lit out and—if I hadn't got in here I should have got in somewhere." The irritability broke through. "I just took a holiday on the spur of the moment. All right?"

"Leaving a note for your husband." He just hadn't noticed that she was annoyed. He was like an inquisitor, oblivious of, uninterested in, her reactions.

"My husband is abroad. On business." When she had said that once, at one of Daphne's parties, the man she had said it to had started to make a pass at her. It was a pathetic thing to have to say. And somehow to say it alarmed her, as well as having undesirable effects on other people . . .

But this man, he was on his feet, looking down at her, suddenly brisk.

"I must leave you now. Excuse me."

"Of course."

For the first time she thought he was hesitant. He said slowly:

"I hope you will enjoy your holiday. I shall see you again." He turned away, then immediately back to her. "So you were—surprised that no one came in to dinner?"

"Of course I was. I'm still trying to think of reasons. If they were invalids and had trays in their rooms they wouldn't have been bounding about the place. But there were napkins in rings . . . Bedroom doors shutting . . ." She had a thought. "*You* didn't have dinner either."

He said:

"Oh, I'm not staying in the hotel."

She started to ask him what the mystery was all about, but he was across the room, pausing in the doorway to tell her that he hoped she would sleep well. He went quickly out through the door and down the path, got into his car on the lay-by and as she watched through the window drove off towards Linton.

Joanna sat still for a few minutes after he had gone, until she heard a sound in the hall. She hurried eagerly to the door, but it was only Margaret.

Joanna started to walk towards her, but she disappeared through a door at the back of the hall.

2

Joanna strolled along the promenade, an infinite regress of weathered wooden seats. The tide was up and the water lapped rhythmically against the wall. It was an attractive sound. There was no colour at all now in sky or sea, and the red and yellow dahlias in the front gardens smouldered as if lit from within. Leaning against the wall Joanna saw other hotels like *Seaview* diminishing towards the centre of the town, the hill which backed the far curve of the bay black now against the pale grey sky. Despite the mystery she was intensely happy. When she eventually looked up at the Window it was almost too much to believe that it awaited her, and she went quickly across the road and back into the silent hotel. She thought as she went up the path that if she saw Margaret or one of the other two women she would ask about the absent guests, but Margaret passing through the hall looked at her so coldly all Joanna said as she started up the stairs was:

"I'm having an early night. Good night, Margaret."

She used the big old-fashioned bathroom across the landing (there were green *art deco* tiles let into the white ones half-way up the walls), then back in her room she stood a long time at the Window, looking out into the twilight.

At last, after drawing the curtains, she got into bed. The room was still not dark and she lay contentedly, learning the shapes and intensities of the shadows made by curtains and dying daylight and the one street lamp which had come on while she was looking out. She imagined the room in the winter when she would light the gas fire and the outside world would cease to exist and the shadows on the ceiling would be warm and coloured.

An anxiety began as to whether she would be there in the winter but before it could grow to any size she was asleep. She slept for several hours, then woke and sat up in one sharp movement, already stretching her hand out towards the lamp.

Fool that she was! If she didn't get in touch with Daphne, Daphne, when she realised that Joanna had disappeared, would get in touch with the police. Or if Daphne didn't (and she would, of course), Nancy Edwards would, or Mrs. Stockley, or even Joe . . .

It took a few minutes' fumbling to find the light switch, and when the light came on Joanna was too eager to start action to protect her peace immediately to notice the new charm of the room in its changed aspect of small light circle and dusky corners. She knew she had packed writing paper, although she couldn't remember making any decision to do so, and when she found it she got back into bed and sat with it on her knees. She wrote to Daphne, and to three of her co-workers with instructions to them to spread the message around: she had been summoned without notice to nurse an elderly aunt who was staying—living—at the *Seaview Hotel,* Linton-on-Sea. She brought in the bit about expectations, which she thought would make Daphne, at least (and she was the most dangerous), find what she was doing somewhat understandable. The aunt had taken a turn for the infirm, and had been told she could remain at the hotel only so long as someone was there to see to her. Joanna didn't know when she would be back, but no one was to worry because she had made arrangements . . .

She didn't think her story out, it was all there, ready to be put down in four slightly varying forms. It was so very easy. It would make her secure and she should have been relaxing, relinquishing again all thoughts of the life she had left behind that morning. But as she wrote the last letter she felt more and more distressed and she realised as she came to the end of it that this was because she had been callous enough not yet to have written to Peter, and she was so sorry for him, that he should have such a neglectful wife. She didn't know when he was coming home, but she hadn't even left him a note.

Moist-eyed, she wrote one. She was slightly surprised at the strength of the phrases which paced steadily across the paper. "I have not forsaken you, my darling." "I think of you, somewhere, all the time." "I worry for you."

But she told him the same story she had told the others.

She put the letters in a pile beside the lamp, switched it off, and lay down.

Now she did feel relaxed, drifting into the absolute silence of the hotel. She wondered vaguely if, much earlier, she had dreamed or actually heard the sounds of voices and feet on the landing, but before she could think about it she was asleep again and the next time she woke sun was slanting from the far eastern end of the bay, a line of it lying across the letters on the table beside her. Now there really were voices and feet near her door and she sprang out of bed. She touched the letters with a finger-tip as she stood up. They were somehow an insurance that the real adventure could begin.

CHAPTER 4

I

The notice on the bedroom wall said that breakfast was served from 8:30 to 9 a.m. Joanna's clock said a quarter to nine, the sounds on the landing were lessening, and she heard and saw nobody when she went to the bathroom. She found herself dressing with almost feverish haste, and it was only just after nine when, slightly out of breath, she stood on the threshold of the dining-room.

She was the instant focus of a roomful of eyes. She didn't imagine that. Every face had jerked round towards her and stayed there, in gestures as theatrical, as thorough, as the voices she had heard the evening before. And it seemed to Joanna that every face and figure in the dining-room was a little larger than life, which she could still only think must mean that until her arrival at *Seaview* she had been giving life only a half look, and was not yet used to direct confrontation.

She was glad her table was just round the corner from the door. She slid into her seat and when Margaret came she apologised for being late and ordered tea and toast.

Although all eyes had been on her as she sat down, and frequently throughout the meal, Joanna found there was not one pair of them that she was actually able to catch. When she thought she had pinned them down they were either sliding past her, or looking at something behind her head, or bent again over a plate. It was the same with everyone, including the two attractive girls she had seen in the garden.

It was quickly obvious that the people were separated from each other at a number of tables only for the appearance of the room: conversation was as much from table to table as between those who were seated together, and the formalities of making acquaintance seemed to be long past.

The conversation was as puzzling as the appearance and disappearance of the people who were talking.

"Whoever would expect Terry to freeze . . ."

"He didn't freeze, darling. You're a long way from freezing when you pretend to freeze . . ."

"Don't say he took *you* in too . . ."

"For one frantic moment I thought the sails had stuck . . ."

"You'd better burst your balloon again tonight, Terry, it went down a treat . . ."

"If you start fooling about with Brenda again tonight, Gail, I'll kill you, I swear I will!"

"Don't talk about killing! How can you! Oh . . ."

It was a theatrical wail, which took all attention for a moment away from Joanna. A third pretty girl, very fair and frail-looking, had clapped her hand to her mouth under a white face mottled pink, and now ran quickly out of the room.

"Oh, hell!" said one of the men, in a tired voice.

The eyes slid back to Joanna, and she could no longer pretend that there was nothing hostile in them, she had the strange feeling that they were holding her responsible for the fact that one of their number had just run out of the room in tears.

For the third time since her arrival at *Seaview* Joanna was visited by the strange sensation that she had moved into another dimension. She even squeezed her eyes shut for a moment, prepared that the roomful of people should have vanished when she opened them again and the place be restored to its silence and emptiness of the night before. But they were still there when she opened her eyes, still furtively watching her.

She took stock of them as they began to drift away. Three of the eight girls she would now be able to pick out but the other five would take a bit of sorting, they were all so attractive. The men would be easier. There was a dark broad man with a tidy beard, who spoke more softly and less often than the others, she thought with a Scots accent. There was a lean elderly man with a lot of lines on his face, whose speech was very camp and who held his hands with a studied limpness. There were a small dark man and woman of indeterminate age and similar sharp features who looked like brother and sister. A youngish man with a mop of fair hair, pleasant rounded features and dreamy blue eyes. A tall thin youth with a lot of very curly hair and blank eyes. An exceedingly handsome couple, she thought in their early thirties, the woman dark and winningly smiling, reminding Joanna of a perfect velvety rose. She saw them as a couple because they sat together and kept being elaborately polite to one another.

She sat on at her table until everybody had left the room.

She knew now that they would snub her and she would rather avoid that. But when she eventually went out into the hall, three of the girls were still sitting on the small sofa there, their heads together. They looked up as she crossed the hall on her way to the stairs and one of them—the blond girl she had seen on the long chair in the garden the night before—started to get up. One of the others tried to restrain her with a hand but she shook it off and went and stood negligently near the foot of the stairs, not barring Joanna's way, but in such a position that Joanna could not have got past without pushing.

"Excuse me . . ."

"Enjoying your room, then?" the girl asked her challengingly, her eyes sparkling. One of the two on the sofa hissed "Gail!" in a stage whisper, but she ignored the interruption.

"Yes, thank you," said Joanna, fascinated and uncomfortable.

"Julia enjoyed it too. Julia was very happy in that room."

"Julia?"

"Don't tell me you don't know Julia."

"I certainly don't." All at once Joanna had had enough of mystery. She must find enlightenment, now, and anyway it was going sour. "Look, could you please tell me . . ."

"Oh, if you want anybody to tell you things, ask him." The girl nodded towards the front door, and Joanna spun round. Her acquaintance of the night before had just come in and was standing watching them. "You ask him, he'll tell you. And he'll tell you what happened to Julia."

"All right, Gail, all right. Innocent until proved guilty in the U.K., remember?"

The man with the fair hair and blue eyes approached them from the opposite direction, strolling into the hall past the notice board. His eyes caught Joanna's without friendliness, but without challenge or hostility. She looked from him to the man in the doorway. She felt baited and impotently furious.

"Someone—please—tell me something!"

"Come for a walk!" said the man at the door. She took it as a command and immediately preceded him out on to the path.

2

They walked without speaking out of the garden and along the promenade towards the town. Joanna recovered enough to notice that the tide was well out and the sands flat and golden, gleaming intermittently with a few pale blue rills. A small late-summer mist had not yet quite cleared, and the buildings of the bay swam together in a hazy dazzle.

The man beside her continued silent, and Joanna thought he was using his silence to draw a reaction. But that didn't matter. She said:

"There were things you could have told me last night."

"There are always things people could tell each other."

"Oh, please!" He was looking at her all the time, steadily. "Don't play games with me!"

His eyes flickered and came back to her with a different expression, less intense, and Joanna had the feeling she had reminded him of something.

"Oh, no," he said, "I won't do that. Sit down."

He took hold of her elbow and they sat down on one of the seats in the sea wall. The small hotel in front of them was called *Heart of Oak.* It had an upper window like hers. How *now,* if she had turned towards *that* window, those years ago? Was life chance, or an inexorable pattern? That was the question of questions, which she could start thinking about behind her own window, now she was free. But as yet—irritatingly, intriguingly—she was not free . . .

"Please!"

He held out a card in a leather wallet. She gazed at it uncomprehending for a moment. He took it away as she recognised the small photograph as his.

"Detective Inspector Neil Carter, Scotland Yard, investigating the murder at the Tivoli." He pronounced the phrase portentously, so that it sounded like a title by Agatha Christie.

Some things fell into place, but not many.

"Murder . . . ?"

"Most foul. Look," he said, "you come to theatrical digs in the high season and you find the best room empty . . ."

"Theatrical digs?"

He grimaced. "Ma Tompkins wouldn't like to hear it called that. And there aren't so many left in her class, these days. But *Seaview* has apparently always taken the summer show people." She went on staring at him and he said, with slight impatience:

"The people staying at *Seaview* are the company at the Tivoli, twice nightly except Sundays. End of pier stuff. Only the theatre's actually in the town, and of considerably more repute than the size of Linton would suggest."

She smiled, and thought it was the last reaction he had expected.

"You know," she said, "I was almost beginning to think I'd strayed into another dimension, they didn't seem to belong to any world I'd ever been in. And the explanation was so simple!"

His expression changed again, into a new sort of intensity which made her wary. He said:

"You're a strange young woman."

"Neither strange nor particularly young," said Joanna, brusque at last from some obscure instinct of self-defence. "But still very curious. Murder . . ."

Perhaps she had imagined whatever it was that had made her wary. He said:

"I'm afraid so. One of the company's stars—there's a very fine sense of hierarchy in this business, you know, like in most—was found strangled ten days ago. You might have seen it. Name of Julia. Just that, but the other name was Wentworth. Versatile, so they tell me. Song, dance, patter, piano. 'Much loved,' the phrase I most often hear. She's number two in the hierarchy—the comedian's always number one. But he let her have the best room at *Seaview*."

He was looking at her sympathetically, and as she exclaimed Joanna realised he was waiting for her shocked reaction to the putting of two and two together.

"It didn't happen in the hotel," said Neil Carter, "it happened in her dressing-room."

"No?" She heard herself give a little laugh. "The room was almost desperately clean . . ."

"Ma Tompkins exorcising any nonsense, as she calls it. Hard luck on her, the whole business, but at least it didn't happen in her hotel."

"So of course they don't like me, they think I'm . . ."

"One of my ilk, probably. Come to turn artiste against artiste. They're a clannish lot. And I must say," went on Detective Inspector Carter, "that I didn't like you at first either. The fact of your appearance at *Seaview,* that is. It just didn't seem possible that it could be a coincidence."

"It was."

"Oh, I know that now."

He said it so confidently, lazily smiling, that she jumped to her feet. "You didn't . . . I don't want anyone to know . . ."

"Nobody knows." He took her arm and she sat down again. He kept his hand on it as he went on speaking. "Nobody knows that they've even been answering questions. But they did. And we now accept that you have nothing to do with Julia or the summer show. Although we don't know why you came."

"I told you," said Joanna, getting up again so that his hand was pushed away. He got up too. "Anyway, now you've established to your satisfaction that I had nothing to do with the murder at the Tivoli, why I came is my own affair."

She looked at Detective Inspector Carter challengingly, and was disconcerted to meet again, less ambiguously, the personal as opposed to professional intensity of his gaze. But as she stared at him she realised that his expression was kind. They strolled back towards the hotel.

"Your husband . . ." he began gently.

". . . is on the continent," she answered swiftly, aware of alarm. He stopped again, and she stopped too. He put his hand again on her arm. "We spoke to your old gardener," he said, "and your daily woman." Her arm jerked under his hand and he said quickly, "Oh, not directly about you, we asked them if they were free to take on more work, wondering *en passant* if the Mrs. Stuart they work for is the Mrs. Stuart who recently . . . 'No? Oh, well, it was just a thought.' You know the sort of thing."

"No, I don't. Your men must have been up early."

"They always are. Now, tell me about your husband." She *was* alarmed. Afraid, even. He was still gentle but his eyes were keen and curious.

"Can we go on walking?" They fell into step again. "I told you," she said, "my husband's an electronics engineer and he travels a lot in Europe. This trip was to Holland and Belgium and he'll be home when he's home." She braced herself. "I've written to him there, so he'll let me know when he's back, and then—I'll go back too."

She fought successfully against the dizziness and stole a glance at Detective Inspector Carter. He was no longer looking at her, he was staring down at his feet.

"I see."

The alarm began to recede.

3

They were once more at the gate of *Seaview*. Detective Inspector Carter stopped yet again, as Joanna was about to enter the garden. He held her back.

"On this case," he said quietly, "we haven't got very far. The inquest was adjourned for police inquiries. Which were duly made by the Divisional police. Came a frustrated lull. Then they called in the Yard. We went through it again. Then my Chief sent for me. 'You're an ideas man, Carter,' he said, 'this case is just up your street.' "

"Sarcastic, is he?"

"Wounded in the *amour propre*. There's a lot of it about just now."

"You too?"

"Not quite yet. You could help me. God, how you could help me."

"How could I help you?" She was fine now, as excited as a child.

"By looking and listening and reporting. Asking innocent questions."

"Then they really will have cause to dislike me!" From the corner of her eye she saw one of the girls come out through the front door and stand lolling against the post.

This time he gripped her arm hard. "Look!" he said. "This is a particularly brutal and nasty murder. The snuffing out of a young healthy life. The innocent won't suffer, but the guilty should. Apart from that, he or she might do it again."

The girl had been joined on the step by the man with fair hair.

The pang of alarm which Joanna experienced this time was pleasurable, like the feeling induced by creepy music in a film.

"I see your point, but you must do something for me as well."

"Anything!"

She disregarded the gallantry.

"You must tell them that I can't possibly have anything to do with the murder—from the side of the law or the victim. Otherwise it'll be miserable for me here. And otherwise—well, I shan't be able to help you, shall I?"

He looked down at her appreciatively.

"You're quite right. Come on."

As they moved forward again the young man with sandy hair who had been hanging round the gate came forward and was introduced to Joanna as Detective Sergeant Diggory.

"You want me inside, sir?"

"You can help to round them up."

Joanna led the way up the path until she was just a step below the girl and the man and then she stopped, checked by their cold stares. Inspector Carter asked them to come inside a moment.

Inside, in the lounge and the hall, on the stairs, obviously awaiting the return of Joanna and the police, were about two-thirds of the people she had seen at breakfast, and at Inspector Carter's request all but a couple of the girls were found and escorted into the lounge. Sergeant Diggory then retired to the promenade, and Inspector Carter and Joanna sat down together in the centre of the room, with the players grouped in front of them. The eyes were as they had been at breakfast, looking, and then looking away.

Neil Carter told them without any prevarication that Mrs. Stuart hadn't got anything to do with the murder. She was simply a person who hadn't been well, had come away on the spur of the moment for a break, made first for *Seaview* because she'd noticed it—recently (his head half turned towards her on the word and she smiled without looking at him)—and they all knew why she had got in. That was all. He knew that on principle they would be suspicious of anything *he* said to them (there was one hollow female laugh at this point, from the girl with red hair), but he begged them out of kindness to accept his word now, because Mrs. Stuart had been under strain and needed a peaceful holiday, and she wouldn't be happy in a hostile atmosphere.

He stopped and there followed a short silence, in which Joanna looked down at her lap and tried to think of nothing. Then the elderly man with the lined face and camp hands said, with a limp wave round the assembled company:

"I think I speak for my colleagues, madame, when I say that you are very welcome at *Seaview*."

"We're sorry," said the girl called Gail, "but when you keep bad company . . ."

There was a bit of general laughter, and Inspector Carter put his hands over his head.

"Thanks," Joanna said to him, under cover of the laughter.

He got up. "You know how to thank me," he said.

"But I'm not to keep any more bad company, and if I do, they'll rightly be suspicious!"

"I'll telephone and arrange an outside meeting. Oh, I'll be back here, but we won't especially notice one another." She thought the private as well as the professional interest was showing in his eyes, and again she felt uneasy. But the eyes of the players were now kind, and stayed with her when she met them. When Inspector Carter said, "So long, then," she was already busy looking round the room, and by the time she looked towards him he had gone.

The fair Gail came across to her and said:

"You'd better meet us, then. Margaret! Will you bring some coffee?" and Joanna sat down between her and one of the other girls on a settee.

CHAPTER 5

I

The girl on the other side of Joanna was the frail fair one who had run out of the dining-room during breakfast. Or was she? Wasn't that girl the one talking to the man with the beard and the Scots accent across the room? Joanna said helplessly:

"I'll never sort you amazing girls out, for a start."

"It's easier than it looks," said Gail. "I'll tell you. Susie on your far side"—Joanna turned her head and received a small careful smile —"has two sisters Sonia and Sandra." She waved a hand towards the second blonde whom Joanna had just noticed, and beyond her Joanna saw a third version of this delicate pale gold girl.

"Oh, no!"

"Don't panic. Thanks, Margaret." When she had set the coffee tray down Margaret made a point of smiling at Joanna. The smile looked far more at home on her face than coldness. Gail began to pour out the coffee. Even the rings on her big brown hands had an outsize glitter. "You see, Susie, Sonia and Sandra play sax." Gail smiled mischievously, not hiding her amusement, into Joanna's puzzled face. "You don't know what I'm talking about, do you?"

"I'm afraid I don't."

"The three girls are an act. Saxophone, one apiece. And Mother came too."

"Mother . . . ?"

"Only she had breakfast in bed this morning. The Fair Sax. That's what they call themselves. The programme calls them a novelty quartet. Susie, you'll have to find a fresh title for yourselves next season. This one's too terrible."

"People remember it," said Susie, in a weak voice. She gave a faint hiccup and her eyes were pink in her pale face. She probably *was* the one who had left the dining-room in tears.

"O.K." Gail shrugged and went on. "So there's three, and although you may wonder which sister, you'll know it *is* a sister, and that's probably all you'll need to know. Then there's me. You'll remember *me.*" She had an entrancing smile. Joanna nodded, smiling back. "I'm a dancer (there's four of us) and I also double in sketches—you know, housewife in rollers one minute, French madam the next. Rhoda—she's the very tall girl with red hair over there—Rhoda's the chief dancer, our boss if we'd let her. Well, we do, because she's our choreographer too."

"You were chatting with her in the garden last night."

"That's right." Pink crept briefly into Gail's brown face. "Clare dances too, she's the skinny one, and the only one who never has to think about what she eats, simply burns it up, I'm insanely jealous."

Joanna looked her over, wondering if she had been insanely jealous of Julia. "You needn't be."

"But, darling," hooted Gail, "it's only because of the Effort! And all the energy I use up, you'd think . . . But no, if I lapse by so much as one spaghetti bolognaise, the scale will tell me next morning. Now how far had I got?"

"The sisters and the choreographer Rhoda and yourself and skinny Clare."

"Very good, and you see, that takes care of six of us. The other dancer is Pam. Lovely and calm. Never gets fussed or untidy. That's Pam. Her sort of blonde won't survive as well as mine, though, if she doesn't already . . ."

Pam had a round face and short wavy hair. She was talking to a pale dark girl with a waiflike look.

"That's Brenda with her. She does an act with Brian."

"Brian?" repeated Joanna weakly.

Gail nodded to the chair backing their sofa at right angles. Brian was the tall thin young man with the curls. He was sitting alone, apparently immersed in a book.

"He and Brenda are brother and sister. He plays trumpet, guitar, trombone and so on and Brenda sings. She's great," said Gail, "voice like cream."

"That little couple I saw in the dining-room—sharp-featured, small—they look like brother and sister . . ."

"You're so right. Dirk and Delia."

"What do they do?"

"They assume a variety of disguises and they—well, they tumble."

"They what?"

"They fall about. Oh, not with laughing. They leave that to us! They dress up as Paris *apaches,* for one example, and they do the dance, and it gets more and more acrobatic. And funnier and funnier. But they never show a gleam. Another time it's school kids. They're great."

"They're not young," murmured Joanna in amazement. The little woman was facing into the light nearby, and her face was shrivelled with lines.

"I know. They're fantastic, really, although they're a bit boring off stage. Always quoting the old days in Vienna. I've an idea they're beginning to feel the draught. Well, they can't go on doing that sort of thing for ever. Not that there's any sign that they've begun to slow up. You'll see, anyway."

"And the husband and wife?"

"Husband and wife?"

The velvet rose girl and the handsome man were still going through the motions of an Ivor Novello romance. Joanna indicated them, and there was a whinny of laughter from the silent blonde beside her which made her jump.

"Not husband and wife," said Gail, convulsed. "But they are a pair on the stage, you're quite right, all old world courtesy and smiling into each other's eyes, and they do tend to keep the image going the rest of the time. It must have got into a habit because there's no public to impress *here.* Oh, there's you now, of course, you'll come and see the show, won't you?"

"I can hardly wait." That was true.

"They're Vincent Bailey and Thelma Hurst," said Gail, "and Thelma's husband comes up on Sundays and Stays the Night. It's sort of funny to see the three of them, because old Vincent still hangs around with them." Joanna's other neighbour whinnied again. "Now, how are we doing?"

2

"You're doing very well," said Joanna, taking more coffee. "What about the blond man with the blue eyes?"

She thought Gail's face softened.

"Ah, you noticed Terry's eyes, did you? Terry's a love. Australian. He's our comedian."

Joanna felt a shaft of interested surprise. She shivered.

"I say." Gail looked at her, studying her for the first time. "You're not really ill, are you? I thought the law said . . ."

"No, I'm not ill," said Joanna quickly. "It's just that my nerves got out of hand . . ." The apprehension which was attached to Peter never left her thoughts of him, although the incidents of the last hours had overlaid them both. Now suddenly she saw them again, as if she was peering down at them through a rift in her mind. It took a few seconds for it to close over.

"I'm sorry," said Gail sympathetically. "Tell me, are you—"

"I think you said his name was Terry . . ."

"I did."

"He doesn't look like a comedian."

"What does a comedian look like?" asked the girl whom Joanna was keeping carefully in her mind as Brenda, throwing herself down in the chair beside the settee. She had a small neat head of very short brown hair and a formidable look of intelligence. "Frankie Howerd? Tommy Cooper? Peter Cook?"

"I take your point," said Joanna.

"I'll just identify us," said Gail, holding firmly on to the initiative, although Brenda looked far too indolent to have any interest in wresting it from her, "and then we'll explain ourselves professionally when you see the show."

"The dark man with the beard?"

"That's Robbie Ross, straight singer. Keeps himself to himself a bit, but he's fine."

"Oh, *God,*" said the blond Susie. Joanna looked with renewed interest at Robbie Ross, sipping a solitary coffee, then realised the exclamation was to mark the advent into the room of a short wide woman with a wide flat face under a crimped surround of glinting yellow hair. The face was yellowish too and bad-tempered, the voice harsh.

"Susie! Sonia! Sandra!"

Sighing heavily but losing no time, Susie got up from the settee and shimmied across the room, reaching the door at the same time as her two sisters. Joanna saw pudgy hands urgently grip the arms of two of the slim forms swaying gracefully in the doorway, and then the four women had disappeared. Redheaded Rhoda cast herself round the table, into the deep comfort of the settee.

"Poor things!" Her northern accent was in strong contrast with Gail's London vowels and Brenda's ruling class precision.

"Who was that?"

"Mother!" said Gail. "Otherwise Mrs. Berkeley. Mother's been in show business for longer than she cares to remember, but she still doesn't think that one myth about it is exaggerated and she keeps those poor girls on about half an inch of leash. It's no wonder they take things so hard."

"We've all taken the lastest thing hard," observed Rhoda, and a silence fell. Joanna looked round at the three utterly different women. Rhoda the most physically extravagant with her masses of red hair and strong features and yards of bead and skirt and great length of relaxed body. Brenda narrow and neat and pale and economical of colour and hair and clothes, her hips infinitesimal in her dark jeans. And Gail, perfectly proportioned, exquisitely dressed, conventionally and perhaps even boringly beautiful if it were not for the strong light of life and will that shone in her brown eyes. Clare and Pam, the other two dancers, went out of the lounge. Pam had a little smile on all the time. Clare looked like an El Greco madonna.

"Do you want to tell me anything about—what's happened?" asked Joanna at last, they were all so obviously thinking about it. Belatedly remembering Detective Inspector Carter's injunction, she watched them carefully. Gail said:

"I'll tell you something about Julia, because I'm telling you about the company and we still haven't got used to the idea that she's no longer a member. Julia was super. Clever and nice and fearfully talented. She wasn't a beauty but she was fascinating and everybody loved her . . ."

"Somebody didn't," said Brenda.

Gail and Rhoda glared at her.

"Everybody in the company did!" said Rhoda.

"It must have been somebody from outside," said Gail.

"The police say no to that," said Brenda.

"It must be horrid for you," ventured Joanna, "to feel that you're all, well . . ."

"Under suspicion?" supplied Brenda.

"Well, yes . . ."

"It is horrid," said Rhoda.

"It's horrid too," said Gail, "to be the only one who isn't!"

"How's that?"

"I'd hurt my ankle. Oh, not badly, but enough to take a night off and keep it up with a cold-water bandage. That was the day. I didn't go to the theatre at all. I wish I had!"

Neil Carter hadn't been exaggerating when he had said they were clannish.

"Tell me about the rest of you," asked Joanna, feeling she had said enough for the time being about the murder. "The older man, for instance, with the interesting face."

"Arthur!"

Even Brenda smiled.

"Arthur's one of the real old school," said Gail. "He's a ventriloquist, and a comedian, raised on the halls. Appeared with every great you'd care to name."

"He has animals," said Rhoda, "rather than people."

"You'll see," said Gail. "Arthur!"

He got up from his chair and came over to them. He waved his limp hands. "Ladies!" He beamed at them. His skin was like parchment and his teeth very white and even. He was a neat man—short grey hair, a small bow tie, quiet jacket, small feet in highly polished shoes. His only extravagances were of word and gesture, and they were considerable.

"Mesdames!" said Arthur, putting it another way. "I am pleased to hear you laughing again."

"Oh, Arthur," said Gail, "that makes us feel that we shouldn't be."

"Alas! What boots it with incessant care . . ." muttered Arthur. He leaned towards Brenda and with swift precision removed an invisible speck from her navy-blue shoulder. "Life goes on." He sighed and smiled. Joanna found something unnerving about his teeth.

They were so dominant in his face she tended to look into them rather than into his eyes and, the teeth being incapable of expression or of returning her glance, even if they had been his own, she found herself with the probably unfair impression that his face was cold despite the range of reactions—wry humour, mock indignation, world-weariness, to name but a few—which passed across it.

"I hope, madame," he said to Joanna, with a little bow, "you will consider yourself in good company."

"Oh, I will!"

She leaned forward, hugging her knees, as she spoke. She felt interested, even excited, and her anxiety for Peter was faint and far away. Arthur's eyes, now she had managed to look away from his teeth, were a very clear flecked grey, like the marbles she had owned as a child. The thin pallor of his face, the way his mouth twisted as it broke into a smile, made her somehow think that his life had been hard.

"You going into Linton, Arthur?" Rhoda had sprung to her feet and was literally twisting his arm. His head was on a level with her broad shoulders.

"You hoping for a lift, Miss Rhoda?"

"Of course!"

"You should walk, you know," said Arthur, "with so much to keep in trim." He gave a mock lascivious wink. He straightened his little bow tie.

"Oh, Arthur," pouted Rhoda, "you know how much exercise I get!"

"Come along, then, ducky. Any more for the *Skylark?*" He included Joanna in his inquiring look, and along with Gail and Brenda she refused. She realised that, for the first time at least, she wanted to walk into Linton.

"Be like that," said Rhoda. "See you later," she added amiably to Joanna, as she and Arthur went out.

"I'll get Brian moving," said Brenda. Her brother was still sitting near them, reading. Brenda leaned over and prodded him.

"Come on," she said, "and be sociable for a moment. This is Mrs. Stuart."

"I should rather be Joanna."

Brian had turned round and was gazing through her. He had very pale eyes and a few unpleasantly active pimples on his chin. Joanna thought he looked a rather uninteresting young man, or perhaps this was in comparison with his sister, who she thought looked as interesting as any of them.

"Brian's a song without words," said Gail, when the brother and sister had also gone. "Makes music like an angel, but no conversation at all. I've never been able to decide whether he's shy, or lazy, or lacking. But I expect it's his views." She picked up the paperback Brian had been reading, whacking it down on the table between them. "Well, I mean . . ."

It was only George Orwell's *The Road to Wigan Pier*. A shaft of sun lay across its cover.

"What are you going to do this morning?" Gail asked with interest.

"I haven't decided." Joanna hugged her knees again. The luxury of such indecision! But she should try and take advantage of being alone at last with the obliging Gail, if Gail would only show less interest in her.

"Nice to be able to light out just when you feel like it," said Gail.

"My husband's abroad!" Joanna heard the sharpness of her voice, and saw it in the flash of surprise across Gail's eyes. She went on, forcing her voice down, "He's away for long stretches, and I got tired of my good works. I suddenly felt selfish . . ."

But she hadn't come away because of that, she hadn't known about that until her arrival at *Seaview*. She had come away because there had been no alternative. Joanna wished Gail wouldn't look at her so inquisitively. If she was forced to say any more she would be dizzy again.

"I'm sorry," she managed, "but I don't terribly want to talk about myself just now . . ."

To her relief the curiosity disappeared abruptly from Gail's face and was replaced by concern.

"Of course, ducky. Sorry. I'll tell the others to lay off, shall I? Well, the less self-absorbed among us. It wouldn't occur to some of them to ask anything about anyone except themselves!"

"If you would. If you could."

"I could," said Gail firmly. "Now, you'd better help us solve our mystery. Although if it really is one of us, I think we'd all rather it was never solved."

"But then you'd none of you ever feel right with each other again."

Gail leaned towards her pleadingly.

"It's happened already. It happened in the seconds after we learned Julia had been killed. And it's funny"—Gail looked uncertain of herself for the first time—"I feel a bit on the outside, a bit as if they—resent me—for being in the clear." She laughed uncomfortably. "It isn't a good feeling, ducky. But the thought that any of *them. Any* of them . . ." She shrugged helplessly. "I don't like that Carter man, but he'd better be quick and take one of us away—or else forever hold his peace."

"I feel as if I'm reading a detective story," said Joanna, "only I'm going to get more involved with the characters than I ever have before. Right from the start . . . You know, I shouldn't feel surprised if some film producer suddenly rushed in shouting 'Cut!' and you were all ordinary people with families and dull little private mysteries, and the summer show—and Julia—were all a film or a play."

"Ordinary people with families . . ." repeated Gail musingly.

"Oh, I'm sorry, I didn't mean . . . Actually I meant a compliment . . ."

"That's all right," said Gail, smiling at her, "and I suppose the life does turn you into a funny kind of a rootless person. Even when like me you've got a mum and dad, and you've had a husband."

"Where do you go in the winter?" Joanna had asked the question before she knew she was going to.

"We disappear like the flies, don't we? No, well, that's just the illusion of the man who keeps still. If we're no longer appearing in *his* town, or the show he learned the name of when it was on in his town, then we've disappeared. Actually, most of us are probably doing a cold weather version of what we've done all summer—pantomime—or the clubs, or a spot of TV if we're lucky."

"Not many of you manage to winter in the Bahamas?"

"You're too right, Joanna, not many." Gail got up with a stretch and a sigh. "It's just as well," she said, "that we'll be breaking up in another three weeks and going our separate ways. Nice if the police came up with the answer just as we were splitting."

"If they still haven't," said Joanna, "you may have to stay on here."

"That'll be fireworks. D'you like fireworks? If you do, you should stay on too. How long *are* you planning on staying?"

"I don't know . . ." It was horrible, how the alarm pounced, out of the clear sky.

"Oops!" said Gail, looking at her. It must be that her face had changed. "You really are . . . I mean . . . Look, I really will tell the others to leave you alone!"

"Please don't do that!" Joanna was just able to laugh. "I should hate to be left alone. It's just questions . . . I don't want to be asked questions. I'm sorry . . ."

"There's absolutely nothing to be sorry about." Gail really did have a lovely smile. "Look," she said, "I simply must be off out. You coming?"

"Thanks, but I'm not quite ready."

"Suit yourself. See you."

It was only after Gail had whirled out that Joanna, alone in the lounge, was aware of the pungent perfume she had left behind her.

3

It was nearly eleven o'clock. After riffling through the pages of *The Road to Wigan Pier* Joanna went upstairs and into her room. She shut the door and leaned against it, glad rather than squeamish to have Julia to think about. Had Julia been frightened before she died? Had she been afraid in this room, knowing she was under sentence of death, or had she gone that last night to the theatre as heedlessly as any other?

Absurdly, Joanna walked across to the dressing-table and pulled one of the little top drawers right out, feeling behind it. There was nothing there, not even dust. And the whole room was as neat and tidy.

She wandered over to the Window. The police would of course have combed every corner of the room, as soon as they knew Julia was dead. What had they found? Not much, because Inspector Carter had said that they hadn't got very far . . .

How would she ever be able to sense any undue tensions in people she hadn't met before the crime was committed, and people whose livelihoods were pretending to be what they were not?

Brenda and Brian were walking away from Linton along beside the sea, Brenda talking rapidly, her brother staring expressionlessly ahead of him. Now he was strange. Too shy—or lazy, or lacking, Gail had said—to compose a sentence by way of social exchange, reading George Orwell and playing a variety of instruments on a stage twice nightly. Perhaps Julia had offended against one of his theories, perhaps the murder had been for an idea rather than an emotion. Or perhaps just the opposite, a man who could be a fanatic in one direction . . .

Perhaps. Perhaps. For Joanna they were all of them strange. Strange that a woman who had spent her life into middle-age doing comic acrobatics in public could be described as dull . . .

Joanna looked searchingly round the room for a residue of Julia, for a clue from Julia herself. But there was nothing there. It was her, Joanna's, room which had been waiting for her, as totally as it had been yesterday. Julia had merely been the last in a line of caretakers.

Yet Joanna wanted to think about Julia's problems and the problems of her new friends, because they fascinated her, and because they helped shut out her own . . . problems? Why should she think she had problems?

Terry Dawson was crossing the road in his short-sleeved yellow shirt, his hands behind his back and his fair head bent. He found the first gap in the sea wall and disappeared on to the sands. Joanna glanced briefly in the mirror, stuffed the letters into her handbag, and hurried downstairs.

CHAPTER 6

1

Joanna slowed down when she reached the front door, and when she reached the gate she stood still, aware of the air on her cheek, cool through the languorous sunshine. Autumn was perceptibly approaching in that obtrusive air with a predominance of gold and brown in the row of small neat gardens which faced the sea. She took a deep breath, another conscious draught of freedom, and rejoiced at the thought of time stretching ahead of her uncompartmented, entirely hers to do with as she would and with no necessity to make up her mind about any moment of it until that moment arrived. Already, what she was going to do with the immediate future was by instinct rather than decision.

She crossed the road, enjoying the sensation of bare legs and sandals, feeling healthy and strong. She went down the six steep steps of the first opening in the sea wall, straight on to the hard sand—the sea must strike regularly up against the promenade.

But now it was a long way out and very calm. Joanna could just see the thin white line of foam which was its edge, across level gold which darkened towards the water and gleamed here and there where shallow pools and channels had formed. To her right the prospect was austere, the sands empty as they narrowed to the horizon, the buildings thinning and fading into the dunes. When she looked the other way she saw an insubstantial town like a mirage under the blinding sun, the pier a white line into the water. There were groups of people lying or sitting or walking slowly along, and dogs with freedom gone to their heads tearing in huge circles, lumps of dark wet sand clinging to their fur. As she turned towards the town one of them dashed past Joanna, a brief cool gritty brush against her shins, and she looked down and saw the sand on her legs. There was only one solitary figure apart from herself, walking slowly but steadily with head still bent and hands behind its back, already a good way off, so that she almost had to run to catch it up, and slowed down to get her breath back when she was within hailing distance.

But she didn't hail Terry Dawson. She quickened her pace again for a few strides and came alongside him.

"Hello!" she said.

He turned and nodded and then went on walking in silence, almost as if he had been expecting her. Joanna was not deterred by his lack of speech and smile. She spoke first not because silence between them was awkward but because there was so much to say, and because she wanted to share her joy in her freedom.

"I think you feel as free on an open shore as you do anywhere."

"I reckon you feel pretty free up a mountain."

He had turned to her briefly again, and this time he was smiling. His smile had that quality of some male smiles, of making a woman feel she is the only person in the world.

"Or even up a hill—so long as you can see far enough."

"You're so right." He gave a snort of laughter. "You been talking to the girls?"

"To Gail, mostly." She turned to him, and he was looking reflectively down at the sands. "Or rather, she to me. She's been awfully kind, but I shouldn't think she does anything by halves. One moment all hostility, the next all friendship. She's been helping me to sort you all out."

"She's a nice kid." Their eyes met. Terry's were sailor blue. "Take a bit of sorting out, don't we?"

"It won't be Gail's fault if I don't get you all right." She said, again without knowing she was going to say it, "If you give me *your* version, then I really should get you straight," and was shocked at her presumption. But before she could retract Terry Dawson said: "Well, now, let's see," as if her request had been the most natural in the world. "You going into town?"

In her head she answered him, "Anywhere, so long as it's somewhere I have never been before," but aloud she said, "Yes," and they continued side by side along the centre of the beach among more and more people, bathing and sunbathing and pottering about the open-doored chalets which now lined the sea wall. Occasionally she turned to look at Terry Dawson. His expression in repose tended to suggest that he was enjoying a tolerant private joke. The sun showed up the freckles sprinkled across his nose and cheeks.

"Well, now," he said at last, a second time, "my version of exactly what? Are you asking about us as a social phenomenon—as if you were on some field work for a course in social studies? Or are you asking about us as people involved in a murder mystery—as if you were Detective Inspector Carter?"

Joanna gave a guilty start at the name of Neil Carter, but her reaction to the questions generally was one of dismay. They could have been a rebuff, even though their tone had been so mild, she had risked one.

She said quickly, hot from exercise and confusion and slipping out of her cardigan as she spoke:

"I'm asking about you because I've found myself among you, and you interest me. Obviously you interest me as you are today, which includes being under suspicion of murder." She waited briefly but he said nothing. "I think," she went on, and heard her voice tired, "I should like to concern myself with you—all of you—rather than with myself just now." She knew somehow she was safe in telling him that she could do with help, that he would take no advantage of it.

"Therapy, you reckon?"

He gave her that smile which must send a shiver of self-regard through the most modest of women.

"I suppose I do."

His instinctive understanding of her need tipped her delight with the morning into euphoria. She looked up at the huge sky, round her at the sea, the hills, the glittering buildings, the people, realising that she was utterly happy, saying to herself of the sky and the sea and the town and Terry Dawson, "This is happening now, and I must always remember that it did happen."

They walked on in companionable silence and the pier ahead of them, which had begun as a white string and turned into a grey one, thickened and grew swellings which were regular round pagoda-roofed shelters breaking the tracery of the iron railings, and ended, above the lazy tide, in a large round pagoda-roofed building which looked like a theatre.

Joanna, her peak of joy already receding into memory, pointed to it.

"Is that your theatre?"

She had asked the question before she remembered that Neil Carter had already answered it. Terry turned towards the sea wall.

"That's the winter gardens, Linton version," he said. "You can sit there at eleven o'clock in the morning, on a canvas chair among a smatterings of senior citizens and pigeons, under a glass dome so that you burn or freeze according to the sun, and listen to gems from the classics."

Joanna was there, in a flash of memory. "I know. There's nothing else quite like it. Do they have a brass band, or strings and piano?"

It was odd with her these days, she recalled things she had done or observed, without remembering any precise time or place where her memories had been collected.

"They have both," said Terry, "at different times, natch."

They had reached the sea wall, opposite another six steps. She preceded him up them, talking over her shoulder.

"What sort of things do you all do when you're not on stage?"

They stood facing each other on the promenade. Terry wasn't much taller than she was. Behind him on a hoarding at the entrance to the pier was a poster with his smiling photograph captioned *King of Comedy*. It was funny in a deep delightful way which made her want to smile rather than laugh, to see that poster behind Terry's grave face.

"Well, now," said Terry, "we act a bit like people on holiday. Walk. Talk. Lounge about. Go shopping." She would never be entirely sure whether or not he was teasing.

"You must forgive me if I treat you like specimens in a zoo," she said ruefully, "but you *are* a bit of a race apart to"—she was going to say "ordinary people" but remembering Gail's reaction she changed it to "people who aren't in the limelight." "It's the glamour. One can't help it."

"I used to feel it," he said, "before I went into the business. Still do, if I see one of the greats in the flesh."

They strolled along the promenade. Several people said hello to Terry or smiled. He wrote his name for a couple of small boys. There were quite a lot of people about but only one ice cream van in sight and the sea food chippy on the front of the pier was part of an elegant iron-balconied terrace with what looked like its original fascia.

"Nice, classy little place, Linton," said Terry Dawson, with Joanna's thoughts. "Not quite Bournemouth, but . . ."

"It doesn't seem to have suffered from development."

"No, I think they've a policy. And it's been easier to stick to with Gawscliffe up the coast taking all the expansion."

He stopped, level with a playing fountain which broke the multicoloured ribbon of petunias in the centre of the promenade. The fountain marked the intersection of a broad thoroughfare lined with trees and balconied stuccoed buildings, some of them shops, some hotels, ending straight ahead in a narrowing ascent behind which were sloping fields.

"The main street of Linton," said Terry.

"Thanks." Joanna found she was no longer looking forward to her solitary exploration of the town. "If you could just tell me where the post office is."

"It's right there." He pointed beyond the fountain.

"Thank you. And for your company."

"Look," he said, consulting his watch, "it's almost twelve noon. Unless you really want to prowl round Linton here and now, how about having a drink and I'll tell you a bit about the show?"

She was as delighted as if she had been a child.

"I'd love it! The only thing I must do is post these letters."

2

The pub was a few doors down from the post office, a building designed on its own even though it was joined each side to its neighbours. It had a pair of bay windows and looked the same age as *Seaview*. It was called, to her satisfaction, *The Lifeline*.

"That's putting it a bit plainly," observed Terry as he held the door open, "for some."

"For you?"

She had advanced even more outrageously out of her character today than yesterday, but she felt that Terry Dawson, with his easy acceptance of all she said, was partly to blame.

He murmured when they were inside, as if thinking about his

reply, "A lifeline is the only alternative to dying. No, not for me."

The tables ran regularly down along the wall, oblong mahogany tables flanked on each side by mahogany settles with wings, so that the effect was of a series of private booths. Terry led the way to the table in the far corner of the room and indicated that Joanna should sit opposite to him. The man and the girl behind the bar watched them smiling, and the girl came over.

"Morning, Terry." She looked with unconcealed friendly interest at Joanna. "A new leading lady, then?" Her smile faded before she finished speaking, and she turned her head away. Joanna thought she had realised that any remark relating, however indirectly, to the death of Julia would come amiss to the cast of *Summer Time*. Terry said gently:

"Not this year, Rose. Mrs. Stuart isn't in our business. Mrs. Stuart, meet Rose."

Rose and Joanna smiled and murmured. Terry asked Joanna what she would like to drink.

"Plain dry martini, please."

Terry ordered beer. The man behind the bar was watching them, all the time he was wiping the bar top and not busy with customers. So was Rose. Joanna hoped it was the lure of stardom, operable on all levels from national to local, rather than the new excitement of Julia's murder. She looked away from the bar and at Terry. He was studying her gravely and continued to do so, undeterred by her answering attention.

"By the way," she said, "I've already asked the girls to call me Joanna."

"Everyone calls me Terry."

She had the idea that even when he spoke to her, he continued with the formulating of some judgement.

"The girls didn't give me the impression," said Joanna, "of—well, hardness, that I'd sort of expected. But perhaps that's just one of the clichés of show business."

"Oh, they can take care of themselves pretty well, and they're pretty quick as a race to look after their own interests, but they're warm. I think you can generalise that they're warmer as a race than girls that do other things."

"Did you know any of them—or any of the men—before you came together for this show?" Neil Carter and his colleagues would have taken care of such questions long ago, of course, but she wanted to know.

"I've worked with Gail before. And once with Dirk and Delia. I *feel* as if I've worked with everybody for ever, by now. That's how you get to feel."

"I can imagine it!"

Joanna herself could scarcely imagine a time when she had not been concerned in the affairs of these people, at least she couldn't imagine it without a sense of desolation, and it was barely a morning old.

"Have you always been in show business, Terry?"

"Well, now, no."

Terry Dawson leaned back and grinned. When he grinned he looked very young, but when he was grave and she was close to him, Joanna realised he was entering on middle age. "I was a schoolmaster."

"That would be in Australia?"

Terry nodded. He drank some beer. He had gold hairs on the backs of his rather small neat hands. A shiver went through her as she thought what one pair of hands out of *Summer Time* had done.

"I came to England to teach, too," said Terry, as he set his glass down. "And I taught for a while, and I met a man who produced this sort of thing. He came to a school show where I was acting the fool and persuaded me to have a go professionally. I didn't need much persuading, actually. That was the end of the schoolmastering."

"What did you teach?"

"Everything to people of all sorts."

"That was Don Juan, according to Byron," she said mischievously.

His eyes flickered. "That's so."

They went on studying each other's faces and Joanna thought of Peter, but without seeing him or feeling him so that the thought drifted out of her mind as it had drifted in, without bringing the alarm.

"You read Byron?" asked Terry eventually.

"I did do. At a stage when my brain was retentive. Not for ages."

It was relaxing not to have to be careful all the time, as she feared she would have to be with Neil Carter, that she didn't offer anything which could be construed as an opening for basic questions about herself. She said:

"The only people who received the same uncritical approbation from Gail as yourself were Arthur and Julia."

It was impossible, in that dark corner, to see if he was blushing.

"Well," he said, in what Joanna now recognised as his habitual slow way, "they deserve it."

"Julia was as good as she was beautiful?"

"She wasn't beautiful. At least—well, it added up. She was alive. That's what makes . . ." He shook his head. "And she was good, yes. You were meaning—herself."

"Yes, I was."

"She was good that way, sure." She thought his voice went flat. But she was so ready to think things. "And a good performer. Might have been great, if she wasn't just a mite too old to develop that necessary bit more."

"How old, then?"

"Thirty."

"Was she married?"

"She said not."

"Was she involved with anyone in the cast of *Summer Time?* Oh, Terry, I shouldn't have asked that!" She was appalled. She couldn't remember the past properly, but she didn't think that she had been vulgar. Terry might have been involved with Julia himself.

With this thought she made herself look at him, and he was gazing at her gravely. "You certain you're not doing a psychology thesis? If you were, it would have been awfully smart to come down here."

She thought he was teasing her but she still felt dreadful. She shook her head, knowing her face showed what she felt, and glad it did.

"Forget it," said Terry. "No, I wouldn't say Julia was involved with anyone in the show." But for the first time since Neil Carter had interceded at *Seaview* on her behalf, his eyes slid away from her. He looked at her again as he said:

"She and Arthur had a sort of public verbal thing going. He was always casting himself at her feet in a little set piece, and she was rejecting him with mock tears. I think Arthur would run a mile from any entanglement, and it was only for the benefit of the groundlings. In fact they did a sketch on those lines in the show, and that started it."

"You mean Arthur isn't interested in women?"

"No, I don't mean that. Arthur was married for years. His wife died. He's got a daughter comes up sometimes. I just think—he couldn't be bothered. Have another martini."

"Oh, I don't think so. I don't usually at lunch time."

"Strikes me you don't usually talk to provincial comedians at lunch time either. You'll have another."

"Yes, please."

Rose was there instantly. People were coming into the booths ahead of them, and leaning against the bar. Several came over and said good morning to Terry before settling down.

"Gail told me Thelma's husband comes up on Sundays and forms a threesome."

"You're too right, he does." Terry laughed aloud and reminiscently, then stopped abruptly and looked down into his beer.

"What is it?"

"Guess I just remembered Julia."

"I'm behaving very badly. Why don't you squash me, for goodness' sake?" She was full of dislike for herself, wriggling in among their sorrows.

Again he gave her that grave, analytical look.

"That's all right. You don't have ulterior motives."

Remembering Neil Carter, Joanna felt more uncomfortable than ever. She switched her line of questioning.

"Have you bathed while you've been here, Terry?"

"Most days. It's pretty good."

"I must try it."

"You should."

She looked at him uncertainly and he smiled at her with such radiance she felt partially restored. She would go on, though, feeling uncomfortable about the role of informer in which Detective Inspector Carter had cast her. As if to make amends, and knowing he would not take advantage, she said:

"You've no idea how good for me *Seaview* will be just now."

"Well, Joanna," he said, and she memorised the way he said it, "you'd better have the full picture. You'd like to go to the theatre tonight?"

"Oh, Terry, I'd love it!"

"Right you are."

He went into a pocket and brought out his wallet, from which he extracted a yellow slip.

"One?"

"Oh, yes, just one. There's only me."

Of course he didn't ask a question, but he was looking at her steadily, and something compelled her to speak.

"My husband and I . . ."

Terry said, then, encouragingly: "You and your husband . . . ?"

"We—used to go to the theatre a great deal." It still wasn't Terry, watching her in silence, that made her go on. "He's abroad so much nowadays, we don't seem to . . ." The muddle, and the alarm. "He's abroad now . . ."

Terry waited a few seconds and then put the ticket on the table by her hand.

Joanna picked it up and they both started talking about lunch at the same second. They got up laughing. Joanna bumped her elbow on the wing of the settle, and looked at the wall as she rubbed it. It was treacle mahogany, fret-worked. *The Lifeline* might be the same outside as it had always been, but the Victorians had made their mark on the interior. Things were moving past the fret-work spaces, on the other side.

"What's through there, Terry?"

"The Public. I'll show you."

He led the way through a swing door at the front of the bar. The other room was a mirror image of the Saloon, without the carpet and with a less colourful and varied selection of bottles behind the counter. Two old men were sitting slumped in the back pew, one each side, as she and Terry had been sitting beyond the partition.

"We didn't hear them!"

"And they didn't speak. Can you imagine! You *can* hear, though. There are a few old stories about things being heard that would have been better not . . ."

The two outside doors were close to each other on the street. The air was glorious.

"Back along the sands?" asked Terry.

"Oh, yes!"

They were short of time and walked steadily, scarcely speaking. It was the hour of the *table d'hôte* and people were leaving the shore, or unpacking picnics. Terry said on the garden path:

"Don't take time to decide about a swim. It'll go past perfection soon."

"Yes." She felt herself lightly brushed by dejection. "I'll swim this afternoon."

"You do that."

In the hall he put his hand for a second on her shoulder before vaulting up the stairs. Gail was standing smiling in the lounge doorway. The gong boomed.

"You look just great," said Gail. Her eyes were very bright.

CHAPTER 7

I

It was a bit disconcerting to meet Arthur on the landing after lunch, wearing a short bathrobe, carrying a towel, and obviously intent on the same enterprise as Joanna, whose appearance also proclaimed her purpose.

"Great minds . . ." said Arthur, standing aside at the top of the stairs with his little bow.

Joanna had wanted to be alone in the sea, but she supposed she ought to welcome the meeting in view of her role.

"May I ask you to show me the best place?" She couldn't call him Arthur, and if anyone had mentioned his other name, she had forgotten it.

"Madame . . ." Arthur twisted his face in a way which told Joanna he considered the question absurdly superfluous. "I am not often so fortunate in my chance encounters . . ."

He checked her on the doorstep, with a declamatory gesture of his arm. It took in the whole prospect before them. "A small town of great charm," murmured Arthur, "I find I shall be sorry . . ."

He suddenly set off again for the gate. Joanna followed. His short legs were very white, the calves round above thin bony ankles. Joanna thought of them on the stage making people laugh, and felt a pang of pity for him.

"You'll be sorry to move on?" she prompted.

He flashed his teeth. "In many ways . . ." A line of dots trailed after Arthur's remarks, as if he was implying more than he was saying. It was a mannerism as marked as the limp yet emphatic gestures of his hands. He led the way briskly through the gap in the sea wall where she had followed Terry Dawson that morning, and set off towards the sea on a diagonal course away from the town.

The sea now was much closer to the wall. Arthur stopped abruptly as if he had arrived at the correct spot by a process of mathematical calculation. He spread his large yellow towel with precision, then removed his robe. His body was thin and white and meagre, hairless, with a sharp rib cage. Joanna felt the pang of pity a second time and looked away while she took off her own wrap, conscious of the contrast between them in natural endowment. Arthur stood while she settled herself on her towel and only then sat down, lowering himself carefully and making her realise that he was almost an old man.

"I'm coming to see your show tonight."

"Ah, the show!"

"I'm looking forward to it."

"Yes, they do." Arthur gave an exaggerated sigh. "But they are pathetically"—he pronounced it precisely, syllable by syllable, like Noël Coward—"unaware that they are seeing a shadow of what once used to be. Once, my dear lady, once . . . the *gravitas,* the magnificently inexpressible honour, of treading the boards! My first engagement, I opened the evening which Harry Lauder closed! The performers nowadays—they are so puny!"

Joanna kept her glance away from his white body. She murmured sympathetically, then experienced a sensation she had begun to recognise: a sort of professional stiffening. She heard herself say:

"But Julia—from all accounts—her performance was larger than most."

Arthur rocked on his towel as he threw his arms out. He gave a kindly, amused laugh.

"Larger than most *today*. Julia had talent, a considerable talent—versatility, too, which is more than can be said for most of the young ones. But . . . perhaps *intensity* is the word I seek. Intensity is a better word, my dear, than size, to describe the old performers. Intensity." Arthur repeated the word with satisfaction. There was a tic at work in his cheek. "And dedication," said Arthur, even more firmly. "In those days if you felt ill, if you had that morning lost your wife, if you were dying, you went out on to the stage as inevitably as you breathed, and gave all you had, and smiled!" Arthur paused, as if winded by the magnitude of the spirit he was describing. It certainly was impressive. "Nowadays . . ." he resumed with another sweep of his hand, contemptuous. "Nowadays if they've got a sniffle they stay away, and if something's upset them they show it. On the stage. Imagine that, dear lady, they show it on the stage! Mark you, producers tend to be soft . . . But forgive me, I am tedious. I momentarily mistook your politeness for interest."

"But I *am* interested. Tell me about your producer. Is he staying at *Seaview?*"

Arthur chuckled tolerantly. "Geoffrey doesn't stay anywhere, my dear lady. He is juggling with four shows in different parts of the kingdom. But he comes to see us regularly. And when we were rehearsing, of course, he nursed us *constantly*."

"Is he 'soft'?"

"Yes, he's soft," said Arthur, "but such talent as there is he has drawn forth. He is an artiste, and recognises artistry in those he is directing. When I say that he is soft, he is looking untiringly for the best in the most unpromising among us. If there is a disruptive incident, if somebody becomes difficult, for Geoffrey they are innocent unless they are proved guilty."

"I hope it will be like that," said Joanna, "over the death of Julia."

2

Warm sunshine was soaking into her shoulders. The sounds of children and dogs came to them, clear and thin. Joanna said:

"Oh, I'm sorry, please forgive me!" very quickly on the heels of her remark about the murder and Arthur, after telling her to think nothing of it, lapsed into silence, staring out to sea. Joanna was silent too, venting an inward fury at her tactlessness. When Arthur said at last, in a very grave voice, "We must not grieve," she was fervently grateful. She said, "No," encouragingly.

"We must not grieve," repeated Arthur. "Nor, I think, must we be too passionate in the pursuit of truth. Julia is dead, and if one of us is led away in handcuffs, she will not appear again. We must bow to fate . . ." He stopped, shaking his head, he appeared to be deeply affected. He rummaged in the pocket of his bathing wrap, produced a clean white handkerchief, and after shaking it out blew his nose with a fog-hornlike boom.

"But," said Joanna, "if the murderer isn't arrested, he—or she—may kill someone else."

"Ah!" Arthur got to his feet, and stood looking out to sea. He spoke without turning towards Joanna. "This is always a possibility, of course, but the man—or woman—who is a murderer, that is, who thinks of murder in itself as an answer to a certain type of situation, must be a very much rarer being than the man or woman who, in one unique instance, is pushed beyond . . ."

"Yes, I see what you mean. But all the same . . ."

Arthur turned to her. He was smiling, his teeth sparkling in the sunshine. "Mrs. Stuart, let us sample the delights of the ocean! Winter approaches!"

"Joanna. Please call me Joanna."

"Arthur."

She was glad she didn't in the end have to ask him his other name, from an obscure instinct that to have done so would have been to hurt his professional pride.

"I must," said Arthur, "approach the briny at a trot, otherwise I will falter at its edge. If I gain a momentum, and concentrate on maintaining it, I will discover that I am immersed. It is merely the initial shock . . ."

He had started to mark time, jumping regularly up and down on the sand just in front of his towel.

"But Terry said it was warm."

Still jumping he turned towards her. "So it is, once one is in. But I tend to feel cold . . ."

He wrapped his arms round his thin body and began to move forward. Joanna scrambled to her feet and they advanced at a steady pace over the level sands. The water did have an unexpectedly chilly impact on her warm skin, and if she had not been set on maintaining the momentum decreed by Arthur she would certainly have faltered. As it was she kept going, audibly choking with the shock of the water against her chest so that Arthur said "You see, dear lady!" triumphantly, with a flash of white towards her, before stopping and submerging. A few yards beyond him Joanna stopped too, wallowing up to her neck in water which was already deliciously cool and not cold, looking back across the road to *Seaview* where, her chin touching the surface, she saw the Window rising above the line of the wall.

She couldn't remember the last time she had bathed in the sea. This time it was a cleansing process, the end of a phase and the baptism for a new, although when she thought too precisely about the phases of her life the alarm sounded and she went swimming away from it until she was aware only of the pleasurable ache in her arms and legs. When Arthur reappeared she beat on the water round her and threw up clouds of spray to express her sense of well-being.

Arthur gestured limply to the shore. Six girls laughing their way into the sea looked and sounded like sixteen. Terry Dawson was in their midst wrestling with Gail. Joanna waded towards them. When she reached them Gail and Terry were just surfacing from the ducking the twining of their legs in the scuffle had brought on them both.

"You're not leaving!" protested Gail.

Joanna realised she was.

"I've been in ages. It's glorious."

"I told you!" shouted Terry.

The girls' hair streamed out behind them like the hair of water nymphs. Joanna recalled with surprise that the first house was at six-fifteen. The edge of the sea, now, was warm round her ankles, but as she reached the sand she felt a small wind of autumn flick up goose-flesh on her arms.

3

"If they don't make it, as they express it these days, on the stage," observed Arthur with distaste, "then they give it up and go into a factory, or on to a bus."

Joanna murmured, prone on her towel. She was training herself to look all the time for resentments which might lead somehow to Julia, but although Arthur had a large one, it was an impersonal resentment against a lack of vocation in the young artiste. And Julia apparently had straddled the line between the young and the old approach, as Arthur admitted that Terry Dawson did, too.

"I could not, with honesty, say that he has the mystique—oh, not the mystique—but he is a trouper, he laments the passing of the mystique he has seen and revered in the ancient greats. Oh, yes."

Arthur had no resentment, clearly, against Terry because Terry, in his role of comedian number one, was the doyen of the troupe. Arthur did not in any way question the authority of Terry, which he recognised as *ex officio* absolute, he merely deplored, gently and with many a sonorous circumlocution, the situation in which he found himself.

"The culprit, my dear lady, is the years. Simply the years. The years which will strike young Terry in due course of time. In our business, sadly, one is partially disabled before one is retired. That is its peculiar tragedy."

His bright eyes and twisted smile made Joanna again look away from him.

"Can't one afford," she asked tentatively, "to let go?"

"You speak of finance?"

"I mean in every way—eventually."

"Financially, if one has been prudent, one should eventually be able to retire. But artistically, my dear lady, the vocation claims every part of a man, his mind and spirit as well as his body and his time, and sometimes the spirit finds it cannot afford to retire."

Joanna was afraid the conversation had taken too grave a turn, and that Arthur would later recoil from the memory of having let her see his personal terrors through the thin guise of generalisation.

She got up. She had an impulse to reassure him, whom she liked, even though she had not yet seen him on stage. He tried to struggle to his feet but she prevented him with a hand on his shoulder. His shoulder felt very bony and cold. She stood looking down at him and he looked quizzingly up at her. He wasn't smiling so the teeth didn't distract her from his keen grey eyes.

"It's extraordinary," she said. "I've been at *Seaview* such a short time, and I've never met any show business people before." Arthur blinked rapidly a few times, perhaps at her use of the cliché. "But I already feel concerned about you all, especially because of what's happened . . ."

Arthur's conversational style was catching, or else it really was difficult to go on from there. He said:

"You are a very nice, kind lady," and picked up the hand she had let drop to her side. He raised it to his lips and kissed it.

"What are you going to do now?" he asked her. Joanna sensed he was ready to be left alone.

"I'm going into town to prowl about and see what there is."

"An excellent project," murmured Arthur absently and Joanna, dismissed, grinned to herself as she walked back to the hotel and went upstairs to change.

When she came down again the Austrian tumblers were in the hall. The woman wore a neat summer dress trimmed with white piqué and carried a pair of white gloves. Joanna's heart sank. Was she never going to achieve her solitary progress into town? But again (she felt an unfamiliar thrill of purpose), she must welcome any opportunity which came her way for contact with the suspects.

She caught the dark eyes of the woman and smiled, and the woman smiled back a little warily. The man was wearing a grey suit. Joanna saw them as the parents in an American B picture, but when the woman spoke her accent was heavily Germanic.

"You are—feeling better, madame?"

The title was quite different from the title Arthur had given her, although it was the same word.

"Much better, thank you."

"That is good." The woman turned to the man. "That is good, Dirk?"

"That is good." His little bow towards her was very stiff, so different, again, from the same gesture in Arthur. She couldn't call him Dirk but in this case she felt she could ask for another name.

"Thank you for your inquiry, Mrs. . . . ?"

The woman gave a little giggle, hardly disturbing the slightly anxious expression of her face. "Fräulein. Miss. That is, Miss Bluemkrot. Mr. Bluemkrot"—a small gesture towards the man, another stiff bow—"but we do not use these days." She sighed heavily. "Everybody . . . please to call us Dirk and Delia, madame."

"Thank you. And you must call me Joanna."

"Thank you."

Joanna had a moment's fantasy that the three of them were glued to the hall carpet, her own feet felt rigidly immovable.

"It is good, though," said Delia wistfully, her eyes on space, "to hear again Mr. Bluemkrot. Herr Bluemkrot. It makes me think of Vienna, just to say the words. You remember, Dirk, the waiter at Rumpelmayers', how if he had sight of us coming in, would come to the door to greet us. 'Herr Bluemkrot, Fräulein Bluemkrot!' he would say . . ."

Joanna wondered if the feet of the Bluemkrots felt as curiously clamped to the floor as hers did. She had to subdue an impulse to laugh.

"You are going into town, Joanna?" Dirk had gently cut across his sister's reminiscence.

"I was thinking of it."

She had so little relish for walking into town with the Bluemkrots she could no longer speak of her intention with the pleasure and certainty she had so recently felt. Nor subdue her reaction in the light of her status as amateur detective.

"We," said Delia, "are to take our usual late afternoon walk. Not into town. We go into the quiet for a half an hour, slowly walking together, so as to be ready—ready in every way, you understand, madame—for the evening in the theatre!"

"I understand." Joanna was smiling at them brightly in her relief. "I'm going to the second house tonight, I'm very much looking forward to it."

"You will, I hope, enjoy," said Dirk. He glanced at his watch, then at Delia. "We must go, *liebchen,* it is already after time."

He bowed for a third time to Joanna, and Delia took the tips of Joanna's fingers and shook them. Joanna had to subdue another impulse to laugh as they all, without a wrench, picked up their feet and walked to the door. In the doorway they passed the velvet rose girl's singing partner. Vincent, Gail had called him. He gave her a warm lingering smile which was utterly impersonal and incurious. Joanna thought he might be a great egotist and then, as the smile faded just before he was out of her sight and was replaced by uneasiness, she thought he might be worried about something. As an amateur detective, she did not discard so superficial and baseless a thought, standing on the step between Dirk and Delia she tucked it away.

They left her at the gate, turning sharply to the right and starting to walk steadily along the promenade. Joanna stood for a moment looking after them, and when they reached the end of the next block they turned at another sharp angle and crossed the road. Joanna had the impression that this was what they always did, every afternoon, at that exact spot. And tonight they would be throwing themselves about a stage. Fräulein Bluemkrot, then, would hardly be carrying a pair of white gloves. How rich and amusing life could be!

Joanna had an idea, as she turned left towards the town and started to walk along beside the buildings, that this was the first time she had found herself with such a reflection.

4

Joanna wandered round the small Marks and Spencer's, where she bought a blouse, experiencing the same quiet contentment with which she had unpacked on arrival at *Seaview*. She investigated a few other shops, before following the rising curve which was the end of the main street, noting with satisfaction the imminence of the hills and the possibilities for walking. Then she came back to the main street and went into an attractive-looking café and ordered tea.

It was while she was sitting there, savouring the comings and goings at the tables with her new sharp sense of observation, that she realised there was no longer a rival picture in her head—the home movie had stopped running. She could no longer see the continuous saga of herself and Peter in the incredibly long ago, walking and driving and moving about house and garden. Peter was now simply a name in large letters followed by an exclamation mark, evoking, unless she was vigilant, increasingly unmanageable sensations of sadness and pity.

The vigilance began to waver as she thought about it, and she was afraid that her feeling of compassion for her husband would make her cry. It was a relief to see two of the saxophone-playing sisters, who had not been of the bathing party, swaying into the café. They saw her and came over and sat with her, and kept up a steady dialogue of chatter which she managed to interrupt only once, to ascertain that they were Sonia and Sandra, and that Mother had insisted Susie spend the afternoon lying down, seeing she had a slight toothache. Joanna would appreciate that playing sax might make it worse.

They were as boring as Dirk and Delia in their different way, but much more attractive to look at. They talked so much they found they had cut it fine and Joanna shared their taxi back to the hotel. Mother was standing in the hall looking like Medusa and bore them quickly upstairs and away.

Also in the hall was the meek woman from the office whom

Joanna now knew was Miss Waterhouse, walking about with a harassed air which vanished when she saw Joanna.

"Ah, Mrs. Stuart! There is a gentleman on the telephone for you."

Inside the box she had to lean up against the wall in case she collapsed. She said, "Peter, oh, Peter!" over and over again before she could pick up the receiver, feeling relief and apprehension equally, then not knowing what she felt.

Eventually she said, into the receiver:

"Peter! Peter! Are you at home, darling?"

"Mrs. Stuart, this is Neil Carter!"

The voice sounded shocked and severe. It seemed a while before Joanna realised it wasn't Peter. Neil Carter's voice by then was pleading, he was saying:

"Mrs. Stuart, for heaven's sake!"

She thought a few moments must have passed. She was all right, although the feelings about Peter were receding painfully. She said:

"Yes, I'm here, please don't get excited."

He bit off an exclamation. "You're sure you're all right? I'm sorry I–surprised you."

"No, you didn't." She *was* vaguely surprised, now. "Are we safe talking?"

"There are two separate lines. This one's direct to the box."

"What do you want?" She was firmly in the present, even though the receiver still trembled slightly in her hand.

"To invite you to have dinner with me. Tomorrow night."

Her reaction was apprehension of a different kind. And irritation.

"You surely can't imagine I shall have anything to tell you so soon?"

"That's not a very kind or polite response to an invitation to dinner, Mrs. Stuart." He really did sound hurt, and she was ashamed of her rudeness.

"I'm sorry, forgive me. But I really haven't anything . . ."

"That doesn't matter. You'll have *some* reactions, even if you're hardly aware of them. And I should like to see you. Will you get yourself to *The Feathers* at Wincaster?"

"Wincaster?"

"Five miles due north. Divisional headquarters."

She said listlessly: "All right, I'll get myself to *The Feathers* at Wincaster. What time?"

"Seven-thirty?"

"Seven-thirty."

The dining-room at dinner, empty of all but Mrs. Tompkins, Miss Waterhouse and herself, in contrast to the friendly, noisy crowding of lunch, did not help to restore her spirits. But by the time she went out to her car, dressed for the theatre, the flowering of her regret over Peter and the intervention of Neil Carter had been safely absorbed, and she was once more full of curiosity and excitement.

CHAPTER 8

I

The seat Terry had given her was on the end of the seventh row in the centre block. The programme carried outline biographies of the players set beside small photographs. Even if the light had not been unfavourable Joanna would have made no real attempt to read them, they were for savouring later in the privacy of her room—especially the piece about Julia, who still smiled out optimistically at the patrons of *Summer Time*. The items had such titles as "Summer Time invites you to the party," "Mirth and Melody," "Let's all go down the Shore." There was a letter of welcome from the producer, a puff from the management of the theatre: *New routines, new jokes, new dances, a laugh a minute* . . . Joanna remembered Terry Dawson's grave face with its backdrop of smiling poster. She also remembered being taken to a concert as a child where the conductor was a distant cousin of her mother's. She had been presented to him before the performance, and the sensation she was aware of now, her thumb on Arthur's photograph, was in line with the sensation she had experienced when the conductor ascended his rostrum amid applause. She was, for the second time in her life, agreeably star-struck. And this time, she would be there when the stars came down from the sky.

The cover of the programme revealed that the show was one of four which were succeeding each other week by week through the season. Listening and looking, Joanna decided that most of the patrons were regulars. One woman in the row behind said she would rather have Arthur's cat than his chihuahua. "It's the cat night tonight," said the woman happily. "And the chihuahua, dear, the chihuahua always comes into show number three," countered another, similar, voice. Joanna craned cautiously round. The two women were fat and smiling and spread in their seats as if deeply at home. Another large woman in front of Joanna said to the man beside her that she could eat Terry, he was so lovely. The woman next to Joanna heard this too, and she and Joanna smiled at one another.

"D'you come here often?" asked the woman. She seemed unaware she had uttered a great comic line.

"This is my first time."

"You staying in Linton?"

"Yes."

"Well, you'll just have time to see the shows through again. I come every week."

"Nice long holiday *you're* having!"

"I live just outside Linton, see."

The woman's eyes were very bright. Joanna had an idea.

"Didn't something happen with the company? I thought I remembered reading . . ."

The eyes clouded, the mouth drooped in an appearance of personal sorrow. "Yes, it was dreadful. Julia—she was the chief lady, oh, she was lovely, dancing and singing and she played the piano *beautifully*—she was *murdered*. You'll see her picture . . ." The woman indicated Joanna's programme.

"I saw it. Who murdered her? Did they discover?"

"They don't know yet. Well, they haven't said."

"There are rumours, though?"

"Well, I don't think so. That *any* of them . . . It's impossible. She was so lovely. They're all lovely."

"Perhaps it was one of the stage hands." Joanna jumped at the idea, and the woman's face cleared.

"There's a good idea! That's who it must have been, one of the stage hands." She said indignantly, "Poor things, it must have been awful for them. They're very close to one another, you know, show business people."

"Do you know any of them yourself?"

The woman said reluctantly, "I couldn't say as I did. But Terry and Arthur were ever so sweet when I asked them for their autographs for my boy." She laughed rather sheepishly. "I felt quite a thrill, myself, when they signed his book."

"I know what you mean."

Joanna felt sunk in duplicity.

"Where are you staying?"

"With friends."

Worse and worse. And telling less than the truth was to tell lies.

Her neighbour was drawing breath again, but before she could speak the auditorium was enveloped in the warm opening chords of the theatre organ. It spread round them instantly, all-embracing, anticipatory, and the woman shook her head with a smile. Joanna settled back in her seat, as straightforwardly excited as a small child at a treat.

The organ played a cheerful syncopated tune as the house lights slowly faded and an orange-red glow stole up the folds of the curtain. As the organ and drums concluded on a noisy triumphant chord, the curtain rose.

The costumes were so spectacular, sparkling in the cheerful golden light, that Joanna approved them for several seconds before really noticing they were being worn by Gail and Brenda and Rhoda and Terry and Arthur and the other familiar faces of *Seaview*. Although the costumes were so striking there were only two kinds: one for the boys and one for the girls. Even Arthur was wearing the gold lamé suit with the cerise cummerbund, and even Mrs. Berkeley was smiling exaggeratedly above a long tight gown of plain gold lamé worn over a filmy cerise blouse. She was the only one of the women to whom it was unkind (although it did not flatter Delia), and Arthur was the only one of the men whom the gold lamé suit (in Joanna's reaction) somehow demeaned.

She realised very quickly that the uniform was the true reflection of a team. In the opening ensemble there was no division into comedians and singers and dancers, the separate acts into which at the end of the season they would split and disappear. Now, on the bright stage, they all swayed to the music, all spun round, all sang and smiled and made up the cerise and gold pattern. The only indication of their several talents was that the dancers danced a more complicated routine and the singers came forward one by one, casually it seemed, to offer a leading voice. Joanna discovered that Terry as well as Robbie Ross and Vincent had a good tenor voice. Arthur's sounded a bit reedy. Brenda's *was* like cream, strong and predominantly low, although it rose effortlessly on its last note.

"We welcome you—WE WELCOME YOU—TO S-U-M-M-E-R-T-I-M-E." No, she wasn't imagining it; Terry, Gail, Robbie, Rhoda, at least, were all welcoming *her*, indicating her, just, with the final sweep of their arms. Joanna half glanced at her neighbour, who was staring at the stage with a fixed happy smile. She probably thought the performance was for her—which of course it was.

A last accelerating kaleidoscope of turning gold lamé forms, and the curtain fell. Applause and organ vied only briefly before it rose again on the bare front half of the stage and another curtain, behind which, no doubt, a transformation was taking place.

Terry, still in his gold lamé, dashed on to a crescendo of clapping. He stood bowing and smiling behind the microphone, adjusting it in a leisurely way as he waited for the applause to die down. He then asked everybody if they were well, and received a vociferous affirmative. This, however, did not satisfy him, and he asked again. The response this time was truly *fortissimo*. Then with the same gentle, slightly apologetic smile (which Joanna hadn't seen him use off stage), he began to tell small jokes in quick succession; or not so much jokes, decided Joanna (having to let one after another slide away into oblivion in order at least to savour a few), as amusingly silly remarks strung on the same meandering yet coherent thread of narrative. He didn't laugh at them himself, thank goodness, as some comedians did, or linger where he might expect applause, he threw them away and hastened on to the next. He had had to go to the doctor because he kept thinking he was a pair of curtains and the doctor told him to pull himself together. "My wife talks through her nose because her mouth's worn out." When she went away for a few days she left loving little notes about the house—on his pillow, in the bathroom, by his chair. But when he went to get his evening suit for a night out, the note on the lapel said: "Where the hell d'you think *you're* going?"

The jokes were all clean, although the last one, which was the funniest (afterwards all Joanna could remember about it was that it had been the funniest), only just, and as he stepped back and bowed in his first real pause, the full radiance of Terry's smile appeared, and it seemed to Joanna that it was undoubtedly, and mischievously, directed to the seat in row G where she was sitting. Whether or not she was right, it was impossible not to smile back at Terry, and everyone round her was doing so too.

Arthur was on the stage with him, confiding a sure-fire way to attract the girls, a verbal formula which he demonstrated with Gail and then with Brenda, both of whom responded like nymphomaniacs. They obligingly stood by so that Terry, throwing himself about loose-limbed in his eagerness, could try the formula, and from each of them he received a slap on the face. The slaps were accompanied by a clonk from the orchestra pit, but from a subsequent pink in Terry's cheek, and obviously unscripted smiles between him and Brenda, it was clear that hers had struck unintentionally home. None of them, though, kept uniformly grave faces where the routine seemed to ask for them, and it was already easy to see that they wore their parts like comfortable old jerseys that they could pull about. When Brian appeared Terry wandered up to him and asked how it was that when Arthur made a certain approach to the girls they fell on his neck, and that when he, Terry, made it, they slapped his face? Brian asked Terry what this approach of Arthur's was, and when Terry demonstrated it Brian fell amorously on his neck and the lights went out and one comic session was over.

In the short musical pause Joanna snuggled in her seat in pure happiness. It was happiness of an unfamiliar kind, and its only conscious thought was that Gail might prefer it if Terry didn't really have a wife.

Terry was back on stage, briefly, announcing Brian and Brenda. Their act was loud lovely sound and melted all thoughts away into sensations. Brian played the guitar, the trumpet, the post horn, the zither, the grand piano which now stood at the back of the fully exposed stage. Brenda announced the numbers in her boarding-school voice, sounding briefly prim, and sang them in a way which sent shivers down Joanna's spine and through her hair, it had the true harsh Piaf note of the French cabaret singer, and with her thin pallor and short dark hair, Brenda now looked rather French. Once she half smiled at Joanna. Brian the whole time was lost in his music.

There was no chance, with *Summer Time,* of growing surfeited on an artiste, or a mood. Each changed before anyone was ready for it to go. There was a comic scene following Brian and Brenda in which Arthur undertook the training of Terry as a boxer. Arthur, in a neat lounge suit, offered an amusing sketch of a hustling manager trying to instil confidence into a less than enthusiastic protégé. Terry wore a silk dressing-gown which he was coyly reluctant to discard, and when Arthur got severe with him and insisted it came off, strip music began and Terry minced round the stage, spinning the cord of the dressing-gown, before removing the gown in a hilarious camp parody of a stripper. It was so good that Joanna found herself wondering if it was possible for anyone to put on such a performance without being homosexual. She realised how little she knew about any of them despite feeling they were her best friends, and this brought a slight clouding of her high spirits.

But then Robbie came on and sang, standing very still and a long way back from the microphone, singing an aria and a couple of ballads so beautifully that Joanna put uncomfortable speculations aside. After Robbie there was a sketch in which Terry, in one telephone booth, failed to make contact with his wife in Linton while a succession of exaggerated characters using the adjoining booth speedily contacted New York, Moscow, and Hong Kong. In the end Terry dialled a friend in Sydney and charged him with letting his wife know that he would be late for supper. This was followed by a lavish ensemble strung on a Dutch theme (windmill, scenic tulips, Dutch costumes that shone in the dark), and then the house lights went up and Joanna blinked round in amazement that the show was half-way through.

2

She went out for a coffee in the interval rather than tell any more lies, and when she slipped back into her seat the Berkeleys were already blowing their saxophones, Mother to one side and at an angle to her daughters, attempting uncharmingly to match the rhythmic swaying of their tall thin bodies. Joanna wondered if their constant movements on stage might have been the beginning of the slight movement off stage one was always conscious of with the Berkeley girls, even when they were ostensibly standing still, as if they were gently and fluidly marking time.

The family were good, versatile musicians and, introduced by Sandra, played several emotion-gripping numbers with smooth sustained notes, some lively jazz, and a piece especially written to display their virtuosity. The girls looked very frail and feminine, which added strongly to the attraction of the performance. Mrs. Berkeley's savage smile was fearsome to anyone who had seen her not smiling. They bowed off to the usual tumultuous applause, and Arthur came on with a chair and a suitcase, followed by Pam in tights and leotard, carrying a small table. Pam set the table down by the chair, smiled her satisfied smile at Arthur and the audience, and went off. Arthur, grimacing with a stage lewdness after Pam, put the suitcase on the table and opened it. The cat's voice, muffled, began before the lid was up, and grew loud and indignant as the large whiskered head appeared over the edge of the case, shaking its ears. It was male, but had a coy way of speaking and used its front paws in the sort of limp, dismissive way Arthur used his hands. Its name was Arnold.

Arthur maintained a fixed little smile while Arnold was speaking, just showing his teeth. The way the cat abused and ridiculed the man wasn't particularly original, but it was funny. At last in self-defence the man produced from the suitcase a small brown ball with prominent, permanently outraged eyes and Arthur's mobile fingers for its mouth. The chihuahua, Clarinda, had a thin seductive voice and Arnold, mollified despite himself, began to get the worst of things. Joining in the prolonged applause as Arthur went smilingly away, Joanna was relieved. He had no need yet for personal fears.

And Joanna had no time for further speculation before Vincent and Thelma were on stage, singing to each other with a sumptuous passion that smouldered across the stage (they sang for much of their act at an agonised distance from one another). They both sang well, from Ivor Novello through Noël Coward to the Beatles. Thelma went off a couple of times, during which Vincent continued to sing towards where she had disappeared until she returned in another, equally gorgeous, dress. As they smiled gracefully away, Joanna's neighbour sighed with happiness. "Those two are in love at any rate," came the whisper. Joanna didn't even want to correct her. Anyway, perhaps she was right.

They were followed by Terry doing a Parisian sketch with Gail, which led into an *apache* dance performed by a deadpan Dirk and Delia which got more and more acrobatic and knockabout so that when Dirk produced a tiny gun and shot Delia and then himself and the organ broke off on a strident unresolved note, it was shocking.

"He used to strangle her," whispered Joanna's neighbour, "they've changed it."

Had someone been given an idea?

The last spot before the finale was Terry's. He joked long enough for Joanna to decide that the special flavour of his act was its mixture of speed and serenity—Terry was so quick, but he was so quiet. Finally he acquired a rose from the wings and came down into the audience and sang with a tender half smile into the raised faces of the women who fringed the blocks of seats, holding the rose aloft. He moved slowly, threatening to stop but not really doing so until he reached Joanna, beside whom he sang a few bars before presenting her with the rose and a kiss on the cheek and vaulting back on to the stage for the last notes of his song. Joanna sat still in astonishment, the rose held tightly between her finger and thumb as she had taken it from Terry, his light kiss a rhythmic throb on her face. The women round her were craning their necks in smiling envy. Her neighbour leaned towards her and whispered again. "I'd always thought it was arranged, but you've proved it isn't. I'm glad it isn't."

Joanna murmured, "No, it isn't," but feeling so dishonest there was no longer any point in worrying about it. The curtain rose for the last spectacular scene, in which the players were all dressed alike in white and silver and came down to the front of the stage in ascending order of their importance, each to a fresh wave of applause, before retiring to right and left. Terry came last, and when the music and the applause had died away he told them what a good audience they had been, asked them to go carefully on the roads, and said goodnight. Then everyone else went off singing, the stage darkened, and Terry moved back and half crouched, half knelt on the steps down which they had all come running. He sang, ruminatively, *The Party's Over*, visible as only a little more than a silhouette, and as his song ended the last of the light went out and the curtain came slowly down. For the first time there was absolute silence in the auditorium. It held until the organist broke it, and then the curtain rose briskly and everyone was there, standing in a row under bright golden lights, to sing *The Queen*. The audience struggled to its feet to join in, and then the curtain fell for the last time, the organist played a cheerfully dismissive number, and it was all over. Joanna found she was still clutching the rose only when it brushed against her other hand. She wrapped it in a tissue, under the approving eyes of her neighbour, and put it carefully into her bag.

3

She dawdled out, because she wanted the people round her to disappear before she went through the door marked *Private* where the company had bidden her. On the other side of the door was a wide warm corridor, and voices in the distance. Joanna advanced along the corridor towards the voices and came out into a high open area beside the stage, where pieces of scenery she recognised were lying propped against the walls. Unfamiliar, drably dressed men and women were moving the scenery. The people from whose ranks everyone hoped the murderer had come. She spoke to a young man.

"The cast asked me to come round . . ."

As the young man pointed to a door opposite, Joanna had the somehow disagreeable experience of seeing Neil Carter appear behind him. But the detective looked at her without expression. He said coldly:

"Come with me."

"Thank you." Joanna turned to thank the young man but he had moved away. She looked into Neil Carter's alert, expressionless eyes and, responding to his perhaps impatient gesture, preceded him towards the door. Sergeant Diggory appeared from nowhere and held it open for them.

They had entered another, even warmer, corridor. Doors off it were ajar, and there were raised voices. Rhoda, in bra and brief skirt, put her head out of one of the doors.

"Rhoda!"

"Come in, come in!" Rhoda's smile faded as she looked beyond Joanna at Detective Inspector Carter. "You were wanting . . . ?"

"Nothing from you just now, madam." Joanna darted him a look, but he was still impassive.

"*Thank* you!" said Rhoda, but he and the sergeant were walking on. Rhoda pulled a face and shrugged and led the way inside the room. All the girls were there with the exception of the Berkeleys, Thelma and Delia, at various stages of removing clothes and make-up. Gail's eyes looked at Joanna through a mirror, out of a face white with cream.

"You enjoyed it?"

"It was terrific! I've never enjoyed anything so much in my life! Every one of you—marvellous!"

"Thanks!"

Joanna thought all of them had said it. All of them looked pleased, where work in progress on their faces allowed her to see their expressions. She would have expected them not to be interested, by now, in amateur enthusiasm. Perhaps that was another show business cliché which was wrong.

"That detective fellow's here," said Rhoda. There was a universal groan.

"What can he want now?" asked Brenda savagely.

"To solve the mystery, ducky," said Gail.

"I can't somehow remember a time when this hadn't happened," said Clare.

Joanna was watching Pam's invariable smile, deciding it wasn't quite human.

"Did Julia share . . . ?"

"Julia had her own dressing-room," said Gail, "off the props room. I should think that's one of the things that make it so difficult for the police. Whoever—did it, could have gone in through the props room, could have been hiding there even, there are so many places, just as well as actually through Julia's outside door."

"What time did it happen?"

They looked at one another.

Brenda said quietly: "She was dead when we were ready to leave."

It was time to change the subject, and anyway she must comment on their personal performance.

"Thanks for seeing me out there. I know you did."

"Oh, Terry," said Gail.

"I didn't just mean Terry. You were all looking, right from the start, I loved it."

She was glad Gail smiled at her.

"Go and see Terry," said Gail, "and thank him. His door's a bit along on the other side. Got his name on. He'll be decent by now."

She went out into the corridor and across to Terry's door. She knocked and his voice told her to come in. The first thing Joanna noticed was the photograph of a thin-faced dark woman on his dressing-table, prominent among jars and trails of cotton wool. The room was quite cosy, with a couch and an easy chair. Terry was at the dressing-table, but got up when he saw her in the mirror. He turned to her with his radiant smile, and she found herself going up to him impetuously, childishly.

"Thanks. I felt I had a spotlight on me the whole time—and then I *did!* Oh, but I should start by telling you how much I enjoyed the show, it was marvellous." She couldn't tell a professional like Terry how good he was, it would sound arrogant.

"I'm glad you enjoyed it. Sit down."

Back inside herself, she sat down a bit awkwardly on the edge of the armchair, feeling untalented. Terry was busy again at the dressing-table.

"I think you're all tremendous," she said.

"I really am glad you enjoyed it," said Terry, squinting at his face in the glass.

"You and the girls all seem to be glad about that," said Joanna. "I should have thought that by now . . . it didn't matter . . ."

Terry whirled round on her. It was the first time she had seen him severe, although she had known from the start that he could be.

"If the reaction of the people we play to, the people because of whom we're there at all, stopped mattering to us, we'd be finished, and rightly."

"Yes," she said meekly, and he gave his abrupt laugh, staring down at the powder-spattered carpet. "Was—Julia's dressing-room like this?"

"Something like it. Come and see."

He held out his hand and she touched it as she got to her feet. He held her hand as far as the door. Perhaps he would have continued to hold it if Joanna hadn't pulled it away. Neil Carter was standing outside the door. Terry asked him if he wanted anything. He looked from Terry to Joanna. She could see the wolfish tips of his canines.

"Not just now," he said after a pause, turning away towards the girls' dressing-room. Joanna walked beside Terry to the door next to his, and Terry opened it and switched on the light. It was slightly smaller than his room, similarly furnished. It was as clinically clean and tidy as the room at *Seaview*. It had a second door. Joanna looked at Terry.

"Here?"

He nodded at the floor near the screen. He took her hand again and led her across to the other door, which he opened. Shapes were outlined by a weak light which shone through a far open door from the corridor. As her eyes adjusted Joanna saw they were piles of clothes spilling out of baskets, racks of clothes, odd things lying about like swords and glasses and padded bras and artificial flowers.

"Props and wardrobe," explained Terry. He went on softly, "Whoever it was could have come in through here."

"Props and wardrobe mistress?"

"Nobody around now. The girls do the running repairs."

He helped her over the obstacles. They were back in the corridor.

"How is everyone else housed?"

"Arthur opposite. The Berkeleys and Delia at the far end beyond the girls. Dirk and Vincent and Robbie beyond the props. Then there's a room opposite the Berkeleys—that is, next to me on the other side—which Geoffrey uses when he's up."

"I didn't see Thelma."

"Quite right. She's officially with the Berkeleys and Delia but rather ostentatiously uses the largest female loo in which to change. She has Julia ambitions but hasn't got there yet."

"Terry . . ."

"Oh, no," he said quickly, "Julia wasn't in her way. They're on different lines."

"Terry, it must have been a stage hand!"

He smiled at her, she thought sadly.

"They say they were all the other side of that door, and heaven knows, they get bawled out enough for coming through it when the *artistes*"—he gave the word a derisive emphasis—"are scrambling to get cleaned up and away. If one of them had sneaked in, he or she'd have been noticed. By his or her colleagues for being absent, and by us for being present. It would have been madness."

"Perhaps it was. Or they might have hidden in the props room."

"It's been thought of. Discussed. Suggested to the police. It's not impossible, but it's dreadfully unlikely. The stage manager's a tartar and there are no passengers."

"The orchestra!"

"Jake and Charlie? They don't have any quarters in the theatre and they're staying the other end of Linton and dash for a last bus.

A less glamorous aspect of the profession. No, honey, at the end of the show it's only the players who don't have to account for themselves. Besides . . ."

"Yes?"

They went back into Terry's dressing-room and she sat in the armchair again, more comfortably. Terry cast himself down on the couch.

"I don't think Julia *knew* the stage staff like she knew all of us. Nothing was stolen from her. She didn't have any views that might have enraged a fanatic. So it has to be because she was Julia, because the other person reacted to her. I ought to offer you a drink," said Terry, "it's traditional."

"No, thanks." She had a sudden picture of them all going off, animated and laughing, to a hotel to drink before going back to *Seaview*. "Anyway, you'll be going for a drink somewhere when you're ready, won't you?"

He was amused. "When we're ready, dear, we'll be going home to bed. We get a mite tired. Sunday, when there's no show, we tend to go to the *Imperial*. Makes a change, and we can still get an early night."

There was a knock on the door and Arthur's face appeared. It looked very tired, the skin more like parchment than ever, the eyes dull and red-lidded. Only the teeth were bright.

"I think we're on our way." He smiled at Joanna, visibly crispening up. "Madame . . ."

"Arthur, it was a wonderful show. I enjoyed every minute."

He bowed.

"How do you go home?" asked Joanna.

"Three cars and a taxi," said Arthur.

"Some nights I walk," said Terry. "Too tired tonight."

"No taxi tonight," said Joanna. "Four cars."

They left the building in a bunch and Joanna had Gail and Rhoda and Pam in her car. Margaret was waiting in the hall at *Seaview* to take any orders for hot drinks. Joanna went straight upstairs. She put Terry's rose into the tooth glass and got quickly into bed, where she lay reading the programme, aware of blessings. It seemed almost too much to have the cast of *Summer Time*, and the Window too. It was only in the night, waking with a start from a dream which was a nightmare even though it was merely about one of the committees on which she sat at home, that her contentment rifted again and she looked down through it at the name of Peter and a confusion of unrecognisable other things. Gradually her surroundings, her memories of the evening, concealed the abyss, but it was early morning before she could fall asleep again.

CHAPTER 9

I

When Joanna finally woke up it was another sunny day but she was aware of a cloud no bigger than a man's hand which while she dressed revealed itself as dinner that evening with Detective Inspector Carter. She was used now to not always understanding her reactions—in a way it was exciting—but she had an idea her reluctance to go to Wincaster had to do with more than her reluctance to confirm that she was an enemy agent. She would rather have forgotten about the evening during the day but she would have to think about it, each minute she was with her fellow guests, because she had promised to help the police with their inquiries.

At breakfast she looked round at them all with a fresh astonishment. Delia was wearing an unbecoming and very ladylike dress in turquoise crimplene and had no reference to the wild-eyed creature who had died doing the splits. At the other extreme Vincent and Thelma were still smiling dazzlingly at each other, handing and receiving condiments as if they were love tokens. Mrs. Berkeley was present, presiding over her girls at their separate table, her voice a harsh bridle on the physical and vocal flutterings around her. Some of the girls, Berkeleys and the rest, yawned rather a lot, looked and sounded faintly snappish. Joanna guessed that some of them would rather skip breakfast or have it in bed, and wondered who had decreed a descent from which only Mrs. Berkeley and Terry could dissociate themselves. Oh, and no doubt Arthur although he was there, eating neatly, chewing each mouthful with great thoroughness. Joanna tried to clear her mind of her prejudice in favour of them all as good professionals and as people who had been kind to her and were enabling her with their presences to shut out unwelcome thoughts.

What on earth had she to tell Detective Inspector Carter? Only that Vincent Bailey kept slipping unconsciously into an uneasiness which showed in his face, then slipping consciously out of it and looking round to see if anyone had noticed. Could she be imagining it?

No, she wasn't imagining it, and she wasn't imagining the sly way Brian's eyes were circling the room, his lowered gaze sliding off one person and on to the next. She thought he covered everyone in the room, systematically, with the exception of herself.

There was nothing else she could find—or of course there was everything: Pam's persistent little smile, Clare's hungry look, Mrs. Berkeley's temper, Robbie's remoteness, Delia's respectability—all could mean so much in the context of Julia's death or it could mean nothing at all.

Now when they caught her eye they smiled at her, except for Brian, who caught nobody's eye during his perpetual progressive observation. Gail perched on Joanna's chair on her way out.

"What are you doing today, Joanna?"

Joanna realised that the cast of *Summer Time*—most of them, at any rate—had taken her under their wing. If she had arrived at the outset of the season, they would probably have adopted her as their mascot. The realisation made it uncomfortable to have to tell Gail that the only plans she had were for the evening.

"Oh, yes?" said Gail.

"I'm going over to Wincaster to have dinner with friends."

Joanna hoped she hadn't at any point mentioned the fact that she was a total stranger in those parts. The trouble with telling lies was that one had to remember one's inadvertent truths.

"Well, we're not much good to you in the evenings," said Gail, preparing to advance into the hall. Even at breakfast Gail gave the same impression of detail in her appearance—the carefully careless scarf caught in the act of flying away, it seemed, by the sparkling blob of aquamarine, the strict outline of the blond hair which allowed for wisps and tendrils, the complement of bracelets and rings.

"Oh, Gail, you say that after last night!"

Again the look of gratification they all wore when they were being congratulated.

"You don't want to come to the theatre every night!"

"I'll want to see all the shows. I gather I'm just in time."

"You are. You are, lucky girl!"

Gail drifted out. Terry followed, with what Joanna felt was rather an absent nod. But that didn't constitute anything she could, or ought to, tell Detective Inspector Carter. As she herself left the dining-room she felt for the first time since her arrival at Linton that she didn't quite know what to do with the hours ahead, she wasn't mentally picking over a wealth of possibilities. She stood for a few moments at the lounge window, looking out on the deserted promenade. Then she wandered into the hall where Robbie was reading a letter and thought with a shiver of alarm that there would eventually be letters for her.

Vincent and Thelma came down the stairs. At breakfast they had been dressed for a smart holiday—both of them in silk shirt, light trousers and cravat—and now they were dressed for tennis, each carrying a racquet in a cover. Joanna thought they were aware that they were greeting her with a kindly flourish, in a way that would do very well if any photographers had happened to be around, but she still appreciated it. Vincent asked her what she was up to that morning.

"Absolutely nothing," said Joanna, not getting quite the relish out of the concept she had extracted from it twenty-four hours earlier.

"Well, why don't you come with us?" suggested Thelma enthusiastically. Her speaking voice was carefully well-bred, but Joanna was not so confident of it as of, say, Brenda's.

"I'd spoil your game."

"Not a bit of it!" said Vincent, rather masterfully. Joanna thought she had never seen anyone who looked more attractively fit. His brown skin glowed, on face and legs, likewise his wavy brown hair. He was strongly built, without fat.

"Several of the others will be coming," said Thelma.

"I haven't got a racquet." But she liked the idea.

Vincent held up his hand. He was carrying two racquets.

"I haven't got all white . . ."

"It doesn't matter. We'll wait for you."

Thelma gave a sweet smile. They were an outstandingly attractive couple. But Joanna, studying them so that they preened slightly under her gaze, was really looking for that uneasy cloud which kept insisting its way over Vincent's face.

"Thanks. I shan't be long."

She sped upstairs happy and light-hearted, found the old pair of white shorts she had debated whether or not to pack, a thin blouse, and some rubber-soled sandals. She hadn't played tennis for ages, but with these people that wouldn't matter.

When she got downstairs again Thelma and Vincent had gone and Clare was looking at the notice board. Joanna wasn't checked for more than a moment, because Clare also was wearing white and carrying a tennis racquet. Joanna was surprised when Clare turned and smiled at her—she thought she had studied every member of *Summer Time* minutely, but it was only now she saw that Clare was the most beautiful of the women, less obviously beautiful than Gail but even more perfectly so, beautiful without any props and through straight black hair parted in the centre and drawn straight back into a pony tail. It was the classic face of woman.

"Forgive me," said Joanna as they left the hotel together, "but you really ought to be photographed."

"I am from time to time." Clare had a soft attractive voice, faintly Irish. "Head and shoulders. I'm too thin for the rest of me."

Joanna didn't contradict. The night before, in a scene where the girls had had bare midriffs, she had noticed Clare's because the rib cage had made her think of Arthur.

"And besides . . ." murmured Clare.

They turned the corner at the end of the block towards the dunes, away from the sea. The buildings in the side road were intermittent, and they crossed over towards a length of fencing topped by wire mesh.

Joanna decided to test her hunch as to what Clare half wanted to say.

"I get the feeling that this isn't the sort of thing—you usually do."

Instantly, Clare's pale face was an all-over delicate pink. She and Joanna looked curiously at one another. Clare's eyes were flecked, tawny, the pupils shrinking into the sun. She said:

"You're quite right. I'm ballet. But Geoffrey asked me . . ."

The gate was in a narrow lane. Clare had difficulty sliding the bolt out.

"Geoffrey?" Joanna had just had another hunch that the pretence of ignorance was one of the first principles of detection.

"Our producer. He'll be here on Monday. You'll see him."

"You knew him, then?"

The bolt came free and the iron gate swung inwards. Vincent and Thelma were knocking up on the nearest court.

"Yes."

Joanna suddenly didn't want to ask Clare any more questions. She wondered if Detective Inspector Carter was ever overtaken by such an access of delicacy. She smiled at Clare and Clare said: "Tell me, do you—" and stopped abruptly, turning away from her and in at the gate. Joanna was puzzled until she realised that Gail must have done what she had said she would do, told them not to ask any questions. For a few seconds she was regretful, but it wasn't simply that she didn't want them, she couldn't take them. And the players had been no less friendly for that. Anyway, they probably made up for it a bit by speculating about her when they were in the theatre . . . She pushed another uneasy thought aside.

2

There were three courts, and Gail and Terry were playing singles on the farthest one. Joanna indicated that she would like Vincent as a partner in case she was a lot worse than the others, but it turned out that she was hardly any worse at all, and that Clare was the strongest player. Joanna's new fierce capacity for enjoyment extended to the tennis. It was won by Clare and Thelma, and then they went and sat on the seat which backed on to the lane.

Joanna reached it first and there were three small girls in the lane who poked a book through one of the diamond-shaped spaces in the wire fence and asked her for her autograph. The new Joanna was tempted to sign, especially as a biro was also proffered, but the real celebrities arrived too soon. The little girls asked if they could leave the book and pick it up after they had been for ice cream and when the other players would have finished and have signed it too—Robbie, Rhoda, Brenda and Pam were now playing on the middle court.

Vincent went with the children to the beach to get ice creams for the adults as well—the little girls were pale and solemn under the unexpected *richesse* of Vincent as escort across the road—while Joanna and Clare and Thelma sat and watched the play which was still going on.

"Is this how you usually spend the mornings?" asked Joanna.

"Probably more often than we do anything else," said Clare. "I gather summer show people tend to play tennis—it doesn't take too long, it isn't *too* strenuous, and it doesn't need too many people." She spoke as if she, like Joanna, was observing the habits of a species to which she did not belong.

Thelma said: "We used to play a great deal at home. Grass, you know. Until Mummy got tired of providing the teas."

Clare said: "Julia was the best player," and Joanna, with the now familiar tingle of getting to work, looked searchingly into her face, and into the face of Thelma beyond her. Thelma's showed more reaction, in the widening of the eyes and the noticeable intake of breath, but Joanna suspected she was being consciously sorrowful. Clare looked thoughtful and truly rather sad, staring at the ground and shifting a foot round to make patterns in the shale.

Vincent came back with four ice creams, which he distributed. Eventually everyone who had been playing tennis was eating ice cream, sitting or standing around. They seemed to Joanna, in the setting of the tennis courts, in their tennis clothes, warm and a bit untidy from having hit and missed tennis balls, more like ordinary people than they had yet appeared. Surely this was the time to spot something, something which they would never give Detective Inspector Carter the chance of spotting? She had reached a position with the cast of *Summer Time* that Neil Carter wouldn't reach in a thousand years. He knew it, of course.

But the only discovery she made while they were eating their ice creams was that Gail was in love with Terry. Joanna realised she had suspected it, in that moment she realised she was sure. The way Gail's eyes followed him even when he walked a few feet to pick up an ice cream paper that had blown away, the way she listened intently to his most casual words. Joanna wondered if Gail was aware of her absorption, it seemed to be something so instinctive. She also wondered, as another new sensation which she didn't attempt to analyse (the new Joanna was more patient than the old), whether Terry was in love with Gail. Certainly, he made a point of giving her all his attention when she spoke to him, but Joanna thought this might be a sort of compensation because he knew he was not so spontaneously aware of her as she was of him. It was impossible anyway to gauge Terry's feelings, both from the quietness of his manner and the temporary exclusivity of his astonishing smile, which, over the morning, was impartial in its distribution.

But it was not the state of Terry Dawson's heart which would interest Neil Carter, beyond the point where it might have a bearing on Julia's death. Joanna looked round on them all again as they gathered up balls and cardigans and lowered the nets. She ran across the far court for a ball and on her way back passed Pam bending down to fasten her shoe-lace. Pam was turned towards the perimeter fencing and her head was bent, but Joanna saw as she went by that the little smile was still secure on Pam's face, even in so private and hurried a moment. How could anyone ever learn anything about Pam, or the explanation of that Mona Lisa smile—self-satisfaction fathoms deep, duplicity, stupidity, the dictates of physiognomy and no more?

So Joanna thought for a second she had imagined it, when Pam called after her, and somewhat urgently: "Joanna!"

When Joanna got up to her she didn't look urgent. She said lightly: "Can I have a word with you?"

"Of course. Now?"

"No, not now." Had there been a flicker of *something* beyond the smile? If so, it had passed. The creamy skin was as pale as ever. "In—private." Pam waited, looking at Joanna without expression.

Joanna said: "Come up to my room when we get back—just before the gong."

"Thanks."

Pam ran off, and Joanna slowly followed. Robbie, Terry and Vincent stood back while the girls went through the gate.

"You know," said Joanna, falling into step with Terry behind everyone else, "you—I mean *Summer Time*—you're old-fashioned in the most reassuring kind of way. You're sort of outside the current preoccupation with being bad mannered and undisciplined, outside trends and politics, and politics seems to be everywhere these days. When I think of you—all—I know there could never be a revolution!"

He laughed abruptly. "If *we* dispensed with discipline, we'd soon be out of a job. We can't afford to be less than perfect. It's cosy for you, maybe. For us it's terrifying."

"Arthur feels it, it's terrifying for him. He doesn't think the young ones do. You, just."

The sea was up near the wall. Beyond its pale blue and white fringe it was emerald green.

"He's right in a way," said Terry. "But even the young ones have to be disciplined when they're on the stage, when they're preparing to be on the stage. The difference is, I suppose, that they compartment it. It's a part of their lives, not all of it."

"Is it all of yours?"

Right from the start she had asked Terry basic questions and he had asked her none. In each case it felt like instinct. They were in the gateway of *Seaview* and he stopped. They looked at one another. Afterwards, Joanna decided that was the moment in which they both recognised they were friends.

"It's a large part of it," said Terry, sounding Australian, as he did more in his brief remarks than when he was slowly defining something. He went on up the path, and she walked beside him. "Arthur," said Terry, "poor Arthur." She only just heard him.

"Not yet, surely?"

Terry shrugged, and radiantly smiled. It marked the end of their private talk, and Joanna ran upstairs. She changed quickly and then stood at the Window waiting for Pam, trying again to be aware of Julia in the room. But she was still aware only that it was hers. She was inclined to start thinking about Peter, but kept being jerked away from him by the thread of excitement which was her expectation of Pam.

She was still struggling between them when she heard the gong. It sounded her disappointment, and her surprise, but there was nothing for it but to answer its summons, everyone at *Seaview* went instantly into the dining-room when the gong boomed. Pam seemed as usual, neither seeking nor avoiding Joanna's eye. In the hall afterwards Joanna managed unobtrusively to stand beside her.

"You could follow me up to my room," murmured Joanna.

Pam turned to her and opened her eyes wide.

"Oh, that's all right, thank you, Mrs. Stuart," she said. "I worked things out for myself."

"I see."

Pam's gaze grew dismissive, and Joanna walked away from her and into the lounge, where she sat drinking coffee and looking round at the cast of *Summer Time* who were doing the same, trying to get over her disappointment. She realised eventually that Pam had in fact given her something to tell Neil Carter. She was aware of the evening starting to reach out and surround her in an aura of treachery. She was glad there was no one in the hall later when she came down ready for a swim, and that she met no one from *Seaview* on the beach—perhaps this was because she walked a long way towards the dunes before spreading her towel. She was in her room when they went down for their high tea.

Joanna took a long time getting ready to go out, moving slowly in bedroom and bathroom because of her reluctance, and when she came downstairs there was only Margaret in the hall, and Miss Waterhouse smiling wearily out of the office.

CHAPTER 10

I

As soon as she had left Linton behind her Joanna felt lighter hearted, curious and even excited. Against her memory of Neil Carter's ambiguous expression she set the fact that since he had found out a great deal about her in a very short time, he must have found out even more about the cast of *Summer Time*—at least in the way of facts—and there was no reason why he shouldn't answer questions as well as ask them. And perhaps—the prospect made her shiver in the warm car—he was now ready to make his arrest and would need no contribution from her.

The road to Wincaster was narrow and twisting for most of the way, between high hedges. The white sun, fading towards the end of its arc, cast a soft light on the pastel slopes and gave the trees long grey shadows which striped the road. Joanna looked round her as she drove, not very fast, aware again of freedom, and once or twice she glanced approvingly at herself in the mirror. In something of an act of defiance of Neil Carter, in an effort to leave him as few loopholes as possible (she wasn't sure what she meant by this), she had taken care to make the most of herself, more care than she recalled taking before in those parts of her life which she could remember. And the sun had warmed the skin of her face and the strain under her eyes was already less evident. Unless it was just that her expression had changed. Joanna pulled a friendly face at herself in the mirror, and then grinned. "You and I," she said aloud, "will be a match for Neil Carter."

The countryside reached right to the edge of Wincaster's main street, with only one housing estate to alert her that she was arriving. The main street was the town—long and broad and lined with a pleasing jumble of old shops, houses and hostelries—and in the widest central part a few cars could be parked in the middle of the road, opposite the eighteenth-century sprawl of *The Feathers*. There was a space.

Joanna saw Neil Carter before she got out of the car. He was standing in the doorway of *The Feathers,* looking negligent. Without seeming to move, he met her in the empty street. He studied her for a moment in silence, then said:

"You look very nice."

She had the feeling this was not something he had intended to say, at least not at this point, not something he had worked out as she was sure he would have worked out the way he wished the evening to go. He tucked his hand under her elbow as they went into the hotel. He was a great one for hands on arms and under elbows.

"This is a very fair place," said Neil Carter, handing her into the small cocktail bar.

"You're staying here?"

"Off and on."

They sat down at a table in the corner. The waiter was there instantly with menus, the barman standing behind him to take their orders for drinks. Joanna accepted Neil's suggestion of dry martinis. They opened the menus.

"You had no trouble getting away, as it were?" inquired Neil.

"None. They were all at the theatre."

"Of course. You've seen the show?"

"Yes."

"They're very good, don't you think?"

"Yes, I do." She was surprised, she had been prepared to defend *Summer Time* against him. But why did she think of him as an adversary? He had to do his job and anyway, there was only one of them that he would harm.

If he could.

"Did you get any further at the theatre the other night?" She thought he was amused by the slight aggression which lay behind everything she had so far said, and was probably showing in her eyes.

He said slowly: "I don't know . . ." then grabbed her arm where it lay on the table. His change of mood and pace made her jump. He said urgently:

"Look, Mrs. Stuart, I'm going to pick your brains tonight!"

"Pick away, you can't find what isn't there."

She drank appreciatively, smiling at him over the glass. She realised she was going to enjoy the evening, with yet another unfamiliar form of enjoyment.

"Even if you don't know it, you'll have formed some opinions. You're an intelligent girl."

"Girl. Thanks." She had never for a moment imagined that it would be she who was being vaguely flirtatious, and he pulling them back to the matter in hand.

"And," he said, "there must be some things you *know* you've learned." He leaned towards her, and she was aware of his pointed teeth. "Tell me, Joanna, and we'll dispose of the business and have ourselves a happy evening."

As she was older than he was, she had half decided she would be the one to suggest Christian names, if an appropriate moment arrived, but there would be no need. She realised she had been flirting with herself.

"I paid attention," she said, trying not to register his last remark and its attendant facial expression, "because I promised you I would. But—whoever it was—has had the best training possible in not giving himself—or herself—away."

"Of course." He was watching her intently, professionally, and he called the waiter over with a click of his fingers and ordered two more dry martinis without taking his eyes off her. "But still, you've noticed something . . ."

She told him about Vincent, hating doing so.

"You're sure about this or you wouldn't be telling me."

"I'm sure he's badly worried about something, or he wouldn't let it break through the façade all the time. But it might be anything."

"Of course."

There seemed a small opening for her first question.

"Do you know anything to his disadvantage?"

"Do you expect me to tell you?"

"I'm not foolish enough to expect anything from you. I would like you to tell me."

She was rather pleased with herself for having absorbed her annoyance at the insolence of his counter-question. And she had done herself more good that way, his face had softened.

"They're making you welcome at *Seaview*? You like living with them?"

"Yes, on both counts. And landing in the middle of such a business—how could I not be curious?"

"How indeed? Well, Mrs. Stuart, I will tell you that I do not know anything to the disadvantage of Mr. Vincent Bailey, unless you consider homosexuality to come under that heading, but that like you I have suspected that there is more there than meets the eye. Not that this is a suspicion which confines itself to Mr. Bailey."

"Vincent is—homosexual?"

She knew she was looking concerned and Neil Carter said curiously:

"You're thrown."

"No I'm not. It's just that—I've got involved with them all. I feel as if I'm reading a detective story."

"I see." He was amused.

"So Vincent is homosexual."

"There is no record of any contact for a number of years. Nor of any heterosexual contact."

"Was Julia at all—butch?"

She brought the expression out self-consciously. Gail had used it in connexion with someone (outside the company) she had been telling Joanna about, and had had to explain it.

"Not that we have found out."

He would surely answer only one more question at the most before he took charge again. She asked quickly:

"Is there anybody else in the company who is homosexual?"

"Not that we have found out. That phrase recurs like a refrain," he said angrily, "and it is assuredly time that you stopped asking me questions."

"But the more you tell me, the more helpfully I shall be able to look for things."

I'm not so sure about that. I think the innocent eye could be more observant."

The head waiter was beside the table, coughing into his hand. Neil ignored the *table d'hôte* menu and chose from the *à la carte* so Joanna did the same. When the head waiter had gone she asked him if he was entertaining her on expenses.

"I don't know yet," he said. Surprisingly, he looked approving. "You're feeling better."

"I am, a whole lot better." She didn't expect him to be concerned with how she felt, she really had cast him in the role of adversary. Yet this was not the first time he had looked at her with compassion.

"Will you have another martini?"

"No, thanks." But she liked the way he had assumed she would have a second, and asked her about a third.

He also asked her what kind of wine she liked before ordering it.

"Tell me anything else you can," he demanded, as the wine waiter went away.

"Oh, yes, there's Brian."

"Brian?"

"Well, he's sort of watching everyone all the time from under his eyelids. His eyes are moving round from one person to the next, especially the people who run *Seaview,* but actually he looks at everyone except me. I don't think he's even realised I'm there."

Neil Carter burst out laughing. He laughed so much he had to wipe his eyes.

"You really are observant, Joanna," he said eventually, with another approving look. "Brian's the union man."

"Union man?"

"I confess that a week or so ago I shouldn't have known what that meant, either. But it appears that each company must elect one of their number to represent them with their union—in this case it's Equity. He makes sure that they're not exploited, that contracts are honoured and so on. The electee doesn't *have* to be a fanatic, but young Brian is something of an activist, I believe, as the current phrase goes."

"Do the others know that? About him being an activist, I mean."

She remembered Gail's remark, picking up *The Road to Wigan Pier* and banging it down.

"I should think they do. They tend to take him less seriously than he takes himself."

"Brenda isn't—like him, surely?"

"There is no evidence."

"Last night I thought he was lost in his music . . ."

"I'm sure he was. The two activities aren't mutually exclusive, although to non-political animals that's hard to understand."

"It's very hard. Was Julia a political animal?"

"There's no evidence. I'm not going to answer any more of your questions."

"All right. I'm sorry I haven't told you anything helpful about Brian."

She was disappointed, because she had hoped her information might have eased his pressure on her, and perhaps because she liked Brian least.

"You've told me that you're a valuable contact. But I knew that already." Again the one sort of intensity was replaced by the other. Joanna waited, consciously blank-faced. "Carry on sleuthing, Mrs. Stuart," he said at last. It wasn't his eyes which changed, it was his mouth. When they were talking business she wasn't aware of the points to his canines.

"I'm thinking all the time," she said. "I'm thinking theories where I'm short on facts. You don't want those."

"It can't do any harm." There was a brief gleam of humour.

"No, well. I've thought—that perhaps someone was too fond of her. I mean, perhaps she wouldn't—respond to one of the men."

"Perhaps she was envied—by one of the girls."

"Have you really not narrowed it down beyond that?"

"My dear girl, we haven't narrowed it down at all!" He sighed, gazing with a frown at the swirls of carpet pattern beside the table.

"*Could* it have been a woman?"

"With all that strong healthy bunch—yes, it could." He was on his feet. "Come on, let's eat. A little more *veritas* may emerge from the *vino*."

2

In the dining-room there was soft slow music from three musicians, and a small square of cleared floor in the centre. Joanna gave an anticipatory shiver. They sat down against the wall, away from the floor.

"Saturday night is dinner dance night," said Neil.

"I hadn't thought it was Saturday. I don't have to remember dates any more—I mean, since I came away."

"Well, it is and you might observe a sort of slackening off among the artistes tomorrow, a sort of *fin de semaine,* if you're vigilant. If they go out in a bunch in the evening, try and go with them."

"I'll try." She would be miserably disappointed if she wasn't invited.

"Have you in fact talked to any of them much?"

"I spent a half hour with the girls after you left," said Joanna, "and then the rest of the morning with Terry Dawson."

Neil Carter's eyes widened.

"Only because he was on the beach when I was," she said. "We walked into town along the sands and had a drink at *The Lifeline.* Knowing I'd been 'under strain'—thanks—they are prepared to divert and indulge me. I asked him questions about them—and Julia."

"And got answers?"

Neil Carter was a machine waiting to devour and absorb the process of Terry's kindness and if possible use it against him. For a moment she hated herself and Neil but he must have seen it in her face and when he said gently: "I think I *ought* to be told," she was able to go on.

"Really only potted biographies," she said, "like Gail gave me in the lounge. Things you're bound to know. Beyond that . . ." Her morning with Terry was a genial glow which she had not really, until this moment, tried to penetrate. "He said that Julia was—good."

"Good?"

"As a person. Decent, I suppose."

"And? Go on."

"When I asked him if she had been involved with anyone in the cast of *Summer Time,* he—"

"When you asked him"—he looked at her in admiring surprise—"You went it rather, didn't you?"

"I told you," she answered, trying not to sound defensive, "that they are prepared to indulge me."

"Please go on."

"He said 'No' but he sort of looked away from me." He might give her something in return for this. "So far as you've discovered, *was* she involved?"

"So far as we've discovered," said Neil, "which is no bloody distance at all, she was not. But they'd cover up for each other, there's the dreadful rub."

"Terry and Arthur," she said reluctantly, "have their own rooms. Wouldn't that have made it easier? I mean, no one would expect them to have alibis."

"Not one man or woman jack of them has an alibi," said Neil gloomily. "Loo, gossip, borrowings, they were all in and out. And it's taken them all their time to remember about themselves, let alone each other. At least that's what they say. She was still wearing the finale costume, by the way, which indicates the murderer didn't lose much time. What more from you?"

"Terry told me that Julia and Arthur used to go through a sort of charade to amuse everybody. Arthur pretending to press his suit and then tearing his hair when Julia rejected him." With her second sip of wine came the warm and pleasant internal acknowledgement that she had had something to drink. The dance music was romantic. "But Terry said it was all for fun."

"They told us about that. We weren't so interested in it, because they were so frank. That can't be all."

"It's all as far as Terry Dawson's concerned."

"In a whole morning."

"There are other things to talk about." His face was changing again and she hurried on. "I'm trying to think what Gail told me. Oh, but they're all such obvious things. Mrs. Berkeley keeping the girls to heel, and Robbie keeping himself to himself, and Delia and Dirk being boring. Honestly, I can't think of anything else. If something comes into my head I'll tell you. And I'll keep looking and listening. All right? Can we give it a rest for a bit?"

With so much of the evening still to come, she didn't know whether she really wanted to give it a rest. But she couldn't think of any more to tell him, although she had an idea there was something.

"How is your duckling?" asked Neil solicitously.

"Delicious. You did well to pick *The Feathers.*" They laughed at the absurd sound of the remark.

"My chief picked it."

"You said you were staying here?"

"I come and go." At last he seemed to be concentrating on his food.

"Do you go to London?"

"Yes."

"Because you work there or live there?"

"Both."

He perhaps looked slightly annoyed by her questions and she wanted to laugh again. The evening's alcohol had certainly taken gentle effect. Neil called the waiter over to pour more wine. He put his knife and fork together. He hadn't really eaten much, he had been playing with it. On Joanna's plate was nothing but a couple of clean-picked bones.

"Come and dance."

The only lights in the room were from wall sconces and candles on the tables. In the centre it was a pinky dusk. Three couples were on the floor, swaying rather than advancing. Joanna was aware, in an access of goose-flesh, of Neil Carter surrounding her with his arms, although he touched and held her lightly. They shuffled in silence, Joanna knowing that her defensive alertness was reflected in a stiffness of her body. Neil must realise it too, he had drawn away from her and was looking at her in amusement.

"Relax," he said.

"You think I'm naïve." She was amazed to hear herself say such a thing, recalling Joanna Stuart in the chair and on the platform. But sometimes, now, she felt naïve, perhaps that was why she had imagined such a reaction on to Neil Carter.

"Maybe in one way, Joanna."

For an instant, for the first time, she felt the length of his body. His grin was lupine, lascivious. He had to show her from time to time the side of him she didn't like, the travelling salesman, little-woman-for-a-night side. But she liked dancing with him . . .

He was looking at her now in quite a different way. He said slowly:

"No, you're not naïve. It's as if—as if you've come from another country, where other customs prevail."

"Yes!" His words made her respect him, they so precisely defined the sensation with which she looked wonderingly round on her brave new world. She smiled at him and his face changed again. He said, almost solemnly:

"I fancy you."

"Well, big deal." Joanna tried, and failed, to imagine what response she would have given in her earlier lives, but in neither of them would a man like Neil Carter have made such an approach to her. She realised she had known he was attracted to her and was glad he had brought it into the open, she would find it easier to parry.

"You don't fancy me, um?"

"It's academic," she said quickly and primly, "I have a husband."

She expected him to sneer, but he was compassionate, seeing her again as a person. He said gently:

"You've heard from him?"

"No. No, I haven't heard yet."

"You don't know when he's coming home?"

"No, I don't know."

The rift again, the terrified glancing down. It made her dizzy.

"Come and sit down."

3

Neil helped her back to the table. She had recovered by the time they got there, having to push between the chairs whose occupants, expansive, had started to lean away from the tables.

"Have a drink." She took some wine. She really was quite all right again, curious to see how Neil would follow up his challenge. But he was still looking at her anxiously.

"I'm all right, really I am. So stupid."

"No, not stupid."

Joanna had the idea he was on the edge of an apology, but she couldn't think what for, the travelling salesman didn't apologise for propositioning the married woman, it made a far better game . . . She wished that Neil Carter would cease to look sorry for her.

"I really am all right. Might I have a sweet?"

The itinerant trolley was attractive. Its attendant waiter was proud of it and made her final choice of a cream concoction into something of a ritual. Neil had some fruit to keep her company.

"How do you stay thin?" he asked her, grinning, being as she thought she would most like him to continue being, neither a detective nor a predator.

"I worry. Oh!"

"What's the matter?"

"Nothing." She had not meant to let him know that she worried, she had not wanted to give him an opening for asking the questions she saw in his eyes. Although, when she thought of it, she hadn't noticed them tonight as she had noticed them in Linton. And all he said now was that all women worried but all women were not thin.

"I'm fortunate," she said complacently. Suddenly she was restored to the mood in which she had been half inclined to flirt at the onset of the evening. She was glad when he asked her to dance again. This time they didn't speak at all, and his cheek lay against hers.

When they sat down she was ready to parry the next stage, but he was a detective. He ordered more black coffee.

"Please try and think, Joanna. Has nothing really crossed your mind that might have a bearing?"

"There was something . . ."

"Then for heaven's sake tell me."

"I can't. I've only got as far as feeling there's something. Something I've meant to tell you. The more I chase it the more it retreats. Perhaps it wasn't anything. I'm sorry to be so irritating."

"You are irritating."

She said, watching him: "You're getting worried about this murder, aren't you? What are you going to do next?"

The coffee came. Without starting to drink it Joanna was stone cold sober.

"I'm going to hang around, and then hang around," said Neil grimly. "Question, and question again. I'm going to charge you to look and listen and ask your own innocent questions, and I'd like you to meet me next Saturday here for dinner again."

"Thank you. Isn't there anything else you can do?"

"I've got a final throw in mind, but I'll wait a bit yet."

It must be awful having to keep saying—to the Press as well as to the Division and his own superiors—that no progress had been made. No wonder he hadn't eaten any dinner. But the Division and his superiors hadn't made any progress either. She reminded him of this.

"You don't think that will help me at all, do you?" he said impatiently. "No, the only bright spot is that there are three weeks yet before they split up, so I've got them captive without having to insist on it."

"If the show comes to an end and you—still haven't made an arrest—can you keep them here?"

"If I have to. But it must be cleared up by then."

"I'll do what I can."

"I'm sure you will." He threw himself back in his chair, smiling at her. A silence fell, the only one of the evening unsupported by the physical contact of the dance floor. She supposed she ought to make a move to go back to Linton, but found herself reluctant.

"It sounds like the last dance." It was disconcerting not to be sure what she was going to say until after she had said it, but it was something else about her new self which she found exciting.

"Come on," said Neil. They went back on to the dance floor. Some of the diners had left and there were fewer fluttering candle points on the tables. The remaining couples on the floor were almost stationary. She was, in effect, standing and being embraced by Detective Inspector Carter. As the music ended he kissed her, a gesture which seemed no more out of the way than a smile.

"If, of course," he said, "you learn anything to my advantage during the week, you'll ring me at once."

She was aware of each point where he touched her.

"If I do. Still at the Wincaster Station?"

"Yes. If I'm in London or elsewhere—if I'm in Linton!—they'll put you through."

They walked back to the table. She was about to sit down but then she saw that he was not. He picked up her bag for her, down beside her chair.

"Time to go," he said, somehow surprising her.

He helped her quickly into her car and slammed the door, almost before she had thanked him. He stood in the road and watched her drive off, raising his arm in a salute.

She thought on the way home of depressing things like Peter's silence and the approaching end of the show and the fact that she was bound to hear from Daphne, if not Nancy Edwards and the rest, but she was unable to depress herself. She felt young and free, and the whole of her channelled into the moment when her headlamp caught a young fox crossing the road and she and the fox both stopped for a few privileged seconds while it gazed with distrustful intensity into her eyes before padding into the shadows.

It was the first time she had seen the yellow front door closed at *Seaview*, but she had remembered to ask Mrs. Tompkins for a key. The door opened quietly and easily and there was a dim light in the hall. Terry was sitting under it, reading. He got to his feet as she closed the door.

"Terry!"

"I was just on my way to bed," said Terry. She could not think that he had waited up for her. "Did you have a good dinner?"

"Very good." She thought she was awful, so why didn't she feel worse? "Did you have good shows?"

"Pretty good, I reckon."

"Are you coming up, then?"

"I'm coming up."

Joanna stopped outside her bedroom door and turned to him.

"Good night, Terry."

"Good night, Joanna."

He drew his finger lightly across her cheek. She could not entertain the thought that he might be a murderer. "You all right?"

"Yes, Terry, all right."

He smiled and left her.

CHAPTER 11

I

There were a few faces missing from breakfast next morning. One of Mrs. Berkeley's daughters as well as Mrs. Berkeley, Terry and Arthur and Rhoda. Afterwards, in the lounge, Sunday newspapers were in evidence, "quality" and "popular" about equally divided. It was extraordinary how a group of people so disparate could engender an atmosphere so domestic. Even Brian had a goodnatured-seeming cushion fight with Susie or Sandra when she wanted to dislodge his feet from a sofa.

The sun, for the first time in many days, was slow to break through, although Joanna discovered from the doorstep after breakfast that it was still fine, and cooler by no more than the due amount of being twenty-four hours nearer autumn. But at eleven o'clock most of them were still in the lounge, and ordering coffee. Gail explained that they didn't play tennis on Sundays. Not from any religious scruple but because they liked to make the day different from other days through all its stages.

Thelma had gone to church with Dirk and Delia. Terry had gone for a solitary walk. Joanna still felt consciously relaxed and healthy. She had been uneasy when she awoke, facing the possibility that she had parried Detective Inspector Carter because she was not sure how far he attracted her, rather than because she was Peter's wife, but as the morning advanced she ceased to worry and carried over from the evening before no more than an increased sense of well-being. And she no longer felt distaste for her role as spy, she had to admit it made sense. She listened for any word about a mass evening exodus, so that she could move towards the speaker and be included.

It was Gail who mentioned it, throwing down an untidy sprawl of newspaper and coming to perch on the arm of Joanna's chair.

"You joining us tonight, then?"

"Tonight?"

"We have supper at a civilised hour on a Sunday, then we tend to go to the *Imperial.* Like to come?"

"I'd love to!"

"Nobody else invited you, then?"

"Nobody else."

"You had a good time last night?" Gail was looking at her curiously, not disguising her interest. Joanna decided that Gail was somebody who really could be naïve, underneath a veneer of sophistication. Or ingenuous would probably be a better word.

"Yes, thanks."

Although she didn't feel guilty any more, she would still hate them to know what she was doing. She was certain that if they did know, they could never be persuaded to believe she wasn't being disloyal. In their world you closed ranks in the face of the enemy, however ideologically pure his motives.

Gail was nudging her. She mumbled a name Joanna didn't catch.

In the lounge doorway stood a small, indeterminate-looking man smiling appeasingly round him. He received lazy salutes. He had thin brown hair carefully and laterally brushed, a long thin neck, and a slightly anxious expression which looked as if it could be habitual. He might have been anything between forty-five and sixty.

"What did you say?" whispered Joanna.

"Herbert. Herbert Wilkins. Mister Thelma."

"Never!"

"Oh, yes."

"She's gone to church."

"She always has, he always gets here too early. Hi, Herbert," called Gail, "I don't think Vincent's far away."

Vincent came through the door at that moment, almost falling over Herbert whose face came to life, his mouth climbing a half-circle which took it briefly into cheerfulness. Vincent sent out a return smile as if he was switching on headlamps, but he didn't sustain it, and as he turned to lead the way to a settee Joanna saw the uneasiness settle back in his face.

"He seems fond of Vincent," she whispered to Gail, in the light of Neil Carter's remark of the night before.

"He wishes he *was* Vincent. He's pathetically stage-struck."

Had Gail answered her unspoken question? She probably had, she liked people and would make it her business to know what was to be known about them. But she wouldn't pass it on to a Neil Carter.

"Yes, I can see he might wish that," said Joanna. "But—Thelma?"

"Thelma was a bit much for Vincent, I suspect. They were partners, and Vincent knew Herbert through his family some way . . ."

"You mean Thelma was on the stage first, and married Herbert *second?*"

"That very thing. I think Vincent introduced them in self-defence."

"And it works."

"If it wasn't working, Thelma would be the last to know."

Gail and Joanna each had a short sharp battle against giggles.

"She's the sort of person," managed Gail at last, "who might have married as a gesture against someone else. Perhaps without knowing she was doing it."

"Against Vincent?"

"Well, yes." Gail's innocent eyes gazed into Joanna's. "They all seem contented enough now," she said.

The morning wore peacefully on. As people exhausted their papers several points of conversation started up about the room, audibility flickering from snatch to snatch and offering Joanna clues if she could grasp them. Only she didn't seem to be picking anything up.

"I've been thinking while I've been sitting here," she said to Gail, who had moved in more permanently beside her, "how cosy and domestic you all are. You might really be members of one family."

"The habit dies hard."

"How do you mean?"

"We *had* got like that before Julia died. Not any more. Not really. Haven't you noticed how they *really* look at one another? Long, unfriendly looks."

"But the whole time I've been here they've all been so nice to each other . . ."

"All that laughing and joking," said Gail, "clowning around and funny routines, it becomes automatic in our business, and when something like this happens it comes in useful. It keeps up appearances, and with no effort because it hasn't got a great deal to do with how we're really feeling."

"But they smile . . ."

"They've acquired the habit."

"But—however suspicious they are of one another—they'd never say anything to that detective, for instance, would they?"

"Oh, no!" protested Gail warmly.

"Not even if they were—certain about something?"

Gail gave Joanna a swift glance of alarm. "I just don't know."

"Good morning, darling!"

Thelma had returned from church and was posed smilingly in the doorway. Herbert jumped up and kissed his wife on the cheek, and Thelma's lavish attentions were seen to be divisible.

"She's the sort of woman who'd flirt with the dog if there were no men around," observed Gail.

2

Sunday certainly was different. After lunch most people went upstairs to bed. The meal had been heavier than it was during the week and Joanna could have gone to bed too, but instead she walked into the somnolent town and, as she had promised herself, followed the main street where it climbed the corner, up past the houses set at angles and interspersed with ancient gardens and entries and decorated with iron balconies and window boxes full of fuchsia and marigolds. The green hill climbed with the road, each side of it, and when the road ran out the track continued and she was on the hillside, hearing and seeing sheep over low stone walls and starting to run about on the springy turf.

She opened her mouth to see how the scream was faring but it was no longer there, only a gurgle of laughter as she whirled her glance round over land and sea and sky and thought of her freedom.

She flung herself down on the dry turf and lay spreadeagled and still, trying to preserve another moment of pure happiness, to prevent it passing its peak of perfection but of course, once recognised, it was not to be held on to, it slid away from her and she lay thinking about the cast of *Summer Time* and Neil Carter's task. She really did feel sorry for him. How could he get anywhere with people like these? The case would, of course, make him if it didn't break him but it would probably break him, even though he was so clever. Poor Neil. She had enjoyed dancing with him, it had alerted her from top to toe . . .

Peter, oh, Peter, I'm sorry. I don't mean . . . It's just that . . .

She rolled over on the grass, to roll away from the abyss. She must learn to help herself away from it, there wouldn't always be a mystery to turn to, a Neil Carter, a *Summer Time* . . . Another memory was filtering through. Her mother had thought she was too young to get engaged to Peter, and had taken her on a cruise. She had quickly become absorbed in the other people on the ship and then, when it docked at Tilbury, the whole thing was suddenly at an end, a whole world, a way of life, bursting like a bubble. This would happen at *Seaview*, on the morning after the last night of *Summer Time*. And then there would be nobody to help her.

But she would still be behind the Window.

Wouldn't she?

Joanna jumped to her feet and walked home as quickly as possible. She went straight up to the office counter and rang the bell. Mrs. Tompkins came forward.

"Yes, Mrs. Stuart?" Her smile was not so bad as Mrs. Berkeley's, but it was majestic.

"I was wondering, Mrs. Tompkins, what happens here in the winter? I mean, when the *Summer Time* people leave. Do you stay open?"

Mrs. Tompkins sighed and narrowed her eyes, as if she had to make an effort to concentrate on something not very important.

"The hotel remains open, Mrs. Stuart," she said, "but I"—she pronounced it "Eh"—"am away a great deal of the time. Winter rates are—er—reduced and there are a number of—elderly people who tend to return. That is to say, they come back each winter to take advantage of the reductions, and then they leave in the late spring."

She meant they were kicked out, of course. That aunt of Joanna's from whom her mother had thought there might be expectations, that aunt had collapsed gratefully each October into her accustomed armchair in the lounge of her chosen hotel, and had left summarily and reluctantly in May.

"So—I may stay here indefinitely?"

Mrs. Tompkins looked at Joanna instead of through her, with a temporary flash of curiosity.

"Certainly you may, Mrs. Stuart. That is, until the early summer of next year, when the cast of the successor to *Summer Time* will move in. You will appreciate . . ."

"Oh, yes, of course."

Peter would be back long before then, long before the winter, he might be back now, and she would have to go home. The acknowledgement was suffocating.

"Are you all right, Mrs. Stuart?"

Mrs. Tompkins spoke rather wearily, looking towards the back of the office and making an impatient gesture, and Joanna remembered that on arrival she had had a dizzy spell at the counter and someone had brought a glass of water. She was amused, and immediately better.

"Perfectly all right, thank you, Mrs. Tompkins."

Mrs. Tompkins' beady black eyes showed relief. There was something cold about her, Joanna thought, despite the generosity of her high bosom and plump upper arms, the tall luxuriance of her hair. Yet she had been on the stage. Perhaps she had been the union woman. Joanna sauntered upstairs, grinning to herself. It was extraordinary how quickly her mood now veered. This was something else in herself she didn't recognise, something else which had changed.

3

The *Imperial* was on the promenade, just beyond the fountain and facing the pier. Outside it was beautiful, a larger *Lifeline*, but inside it was merely warm comfortable sub-Hilton, like any well-appointed modern hotel. The head barman of the Ice Bucket Bar seemed relieved as well as pleased to welcome the party from the theatre, and several people drifted in from the lounge in their wake. Somewhere on the threshold of the bar Joanna was again asked for her autograph, and shook her head with a smile following the example of Gail and Rhoda.

They needed three tables, pushed together. The head barman and his assistant wore their eyes slightly down when they spoke to anybody from the Tivoli group, even when simply taking their orders, which must be because of Julia's death—there was nothing in the demeanour of the party to invite deference and of course, this must be the first time they had come in since the murder. Joanna found herself between Robbie and Rhoda. The awareness of an old order which she had felt on leaving the tennis courts, when Terry and Robbie and Vincent had stood aside for the girls to go through the gate, was revived as Terry, then Robbie, then Dirk, then Arthur, then Vincent, then even Brian, bought drinks and her own attempts were frustrated.

Joanna raised her first glass to the circle of them, recalling Gail's phrase of the morning. "Long, unfriendly looks." She couldn't see them, she could see only a readiness to let themselves go, and that the drinks were being got in rather quickly—perhaps more quickly than on the Sunday nights when Julia had been with them? Joanna noticed Terry's face flushed for the first time. Delia's laugh began to rise in a regular neighing snicker. Brian talked a lot and argumentatively, catching hold of the men by the lapel or the stuff of the pullover when he spoke to them and hovering his hectoring hand towards the women's bosoms, dropping it just in time. Rhoda and Brenda crossed and uncrossed their legs with increasing frequency (the one extravagantly, slouched in her chair, the other economically, very upright and knobby). Gail tended to look pleadingly at Terry and even Robbie spoke at length into Joanna's ear of an old nanny who had greatly influenced his childhood. Joanna, too, was aware eventually that she had had several drinks, and grew self-consciously happy. She thought she and Pam and Arthur were the only three of them not to show their degree of relaxation, then realised that she had assured Robbie of the same sentiment three times, with increasing *gravitas*. This made her want to laugh, and she had a little difficulty in controlling herself. Apparently she wasn't entirely successful, because Terry leaned over and asked her what the joke was. She told him there wasn't one, she was just very happy. She raised her voice so that they all heard her, and said it again. She went on to say that she was happy because they were all so kind to her, that she was as fond of them all as if she had known them for years rather than days.

Terry didn't actually say anything in response to her little speech, but she knew he was looking at her with affection. She smiled at him, privately, after she had smiled round on everyone else, aware that she had a special affection for him over and above the evening's drinking and over and above her affection and concern for the rest of them. It was an awareness that brought nothing but a gentle pleasure. Sometime later, on her way back from the loo, she saw Terry standing in the path she must take over the purple carpet to get back to her seat, and she was going to run up to him precipitately and squeeze his arm, until she noticed the expression on his face, and that Vincent was approaching from the other direction. All at once, without any conscious thought towards it, she was the spy, cool-headed and sober. She found herself moving carefully behind a large screen of potted palms which brought her within a few feet of the two men yet hid her completely from them and, when she had moved round a bit further so that she was against a wall, from anyone else who should also take the route from the ladies' room back towards the Ice Bucket.

Terry and Vincent stood looking at each other, Vincent's mask gone, each face wary and concerned. Terry said at last:

"Well?"

"I must talk to you."

"I'd like to talk to you, mate."

"It's too risky at *Seaview* . . ."

"Walk along the sands with me."

"You know I don't walk. Comment again . . ."

"All right. Meet me in *The Lifeline*."

"But everyone . . ."

"Not at 11:30, not before twelve. See me there at 11:30 in the morning, my table."

"Thanks. Terry, I think I ought . . ."

"Save it. Save it. Pull yourself together now, and come back."

"I'm going to get some air."

Vincent half put his hand out towards Terry. His face was ghastly, and more so as, under Terry's frowning gaze, he offered a gleaming parody of his customary smile. But Terry said: "That's the ticket!" and went back to the bar.

Joanna sidled out from behind the palms and slowly followed him. She sat down. She looked across at him and remembered the striptease on the stage and Vincent's hand half out towards him and the anxiety in his face when he had been standing looking at Vincent.

"I say, are you all right?"

It was really too infuriating and boring of her, to have yet another dizzy spell. She tried to tell Rhoda she was all right but Rhoda thrust a hand mirror in front of her face and it was dead white with black eyes. They were all looking at her and she faltered out that she didn't really think it was what she had had to drink and Terry said severely he was sure it wasn't and he was going to take her home. Gail started to offer to go with them and Terry cut her short and then Joanna wanted to cry, she felt so sorry for Gail with her bright eyes and brave smile. It *was* the drink of course, partly. The doorman called them a taxi. In the back of it she lay inside Terry's arm, knowing it didn't matter what his propensities were, it only mattered that he existed. They didn't talk.

She stood by, restored, while he paid off the taxi. She didn't need the arm he gave her up the path, across the hall, up the stairs.

"I've spoilt your evening for nothing," she said, outside her door.

He twisted a piece of her hair in his fingers, smiling at her. For that moment he looked free of anxiety.

"I had had enough, and so had you."

"Yes, I had. I shall get stronger."

"You will."

The sense of sweetness swamped all possibility of worry, and she got quickly into bed and went to sleep.

CHAPTER 12

I

Joanna rang Neil Carter from a telephone alcove on the first floor of Linton's one department store at half-past nine the next morning. They found him for her very quickly and she started off at once on her information, businesslike, and was surprised when he interrupted to ask her how she was. She could think of Neil Carter in a number of different ways, and the part of him which went with the query was as far from her mind then as the part which made her selfconscious.

Because the telephone was so exposed she felt she must mutter, her back against the wall and looking warily out across Toys and Baby Linen (at least these were unlikely to be of premier interest to the cast of *Summer Time* and at least the other two alcoves were empty). Neil Carter asked her to speak up, but when she said she couldn't his own background noises of conversation and typing fell abruptly silent.

"Begin again."

"Vincent Bailey and Terry Dawson are meeting in *The Lifeline* at half past eleven this morning to discuss something they apparently can't discuss in the hotel. Or even on the beach, because Vincent said it would cause talk if they were seen walking together." His knowing chuckle kindled a sharp little flame of anger. "Because Vincent doesn't walk," she said distastefully.

"That's all right," said Neil Carter, infuriatingly placatory. "What something was it?"

"I don't know. I just heard them make the appointment."

"From behind a convenient potted palm."

"From behind a convenient potted palm! The *Imperial*'s most luxuriant. Last night. Vincent was more agitated than ever and Terry seemed—as anxious to talk to him as he was to talk to Terry."

"And *The Lifeline*, you say?"

"Yes."

When she had started the conversation she had been going to tell Neil of the set-up in *The Lifeline*, of the Public running along beside the Saloon and the opportunities for sound and vision between them. But while she had been talking a plan had been forming in her head and now it was ready. Its success might be contingent on saying no more to Neil Carter.

"Right you are," said Neil. "Thanks. Ring me again of course if there's anything more."

"Of course."

"If not, I'll see you Saturday."

"Saturday."

A man was dialling on the next-door telephone as she rang off. Through Baby Linen and into Young Fashions she encountered Mrs. Berkeley and her three daughters. One girl, a little apart from the mother and the other two, was apparently examining the sleeve of a blouse, but Joanna touched her arm and as she looked up it was obvious that she was trying to subdue tears. Joanna thought it was Susie, but she wasn't entirely sure.

The girl said in a low voice, twisting the sleeve in her hand: "I hate her."

Her pale blue eyes with their pink surrounds were blazing. "I hate her," she said again, "I could kill her . . ."

Her hand flew to her mouth but the check was so brief Joanna wondered afterwards if she had imagined it. "Sometimes I *could* kill her," said the daughter Joanna thought was Susie, defiantly.

"You don't mean that."

"I certainly do. If there's a second tragedy in the theatre," said the girl, on a resentful hiccup, "it'll be easier to solve than the first one."

"Susie! Susie! Look sharp there!"

Mrs. Berkeley saw Joanna as she was in the act of laying an ungentle hand on her daughter's arm. She offered a shortened version of her stage smile. Sandra and Sonia were in attendance, dry-eyed but sullen. Mrs. Berkeley smiled her terrible smile again and moved away, the girls swaying close behind her. Susie turned round as they reached the doors and looked meaningly at Joanna.

Joanna wandered round the department, pushing clothes along racks without looking at them. There was certainly provocation for the Berkeley girls, but with equal certainty there had been real hatred in Susie's face. Perhaps she had hated Julia, too.

Perhaps. Perhaps.

Joanna found it impossible to take in what goods were for sale, even in her favourite departments. She went and had a coffee in the restaurant of the store, hoping it was less of a haunt for the *Summer Time* people than the *Marigold*—it was certainly much less attractive—and saw no one she knew.

When she had finished her coffee she bought a large floppy sun hat in a William Morris print and spent a half hour walking up the hillside. She put the hat on, and her sunglasses, as she turned the bend back into the main street. She paused and adjusted her shoe strap outside the door of *The Lifeline*'s public bar. The immediate area held no familiar figures. As she pushed open the door she half hoped that two old men would be sitting in the vital places, so that her plan would be rendered inoperable, but there was one old man only, with his back to the door so that she was able to hasten up to the top of the dim mahogany room and squeeze into its remotest corner. The old man, behind a pint of mild, made her jump by saying good morning, she had thought his weak eyes were looking through her. She murmured a response and pulled down the wavy brim of her new hat. No one else paid her any attention except the barman, who was there instantly, there was so little business, and she ordered a ginger ale.

It was eleven twenty-five. Joanna shifted in her seat, and had a sudden short-lived vision of Vincent's unguarded profile, gleaming with perspiration, as Vincent took his seat beside her, separated from her by no more than the width of the Victorian partition. It seemed that he was so far alone . . .

"Forgive me if I disturb you for a moment."

Neil Carter was standing over the old man, trying to combine clarity of utterance with keeping his voice down. Joanna's initial unpleasant surprise was followed by amusement and a sense of superiority. Especially as Neil Carter had clearly not recognised her, and had decided the old man was a softer option.

"Eh?"

Neil repeated himself, sacrificing some of the *pianissimo* in the overriding interest of getting heard. "I think I left a book down on the floor by the wall . . ." he went on, his voice desperately polite, his face, above the old man's line of vision, twisted in irritation.

The old man shook his head and Joanna saw Neil's fists clench. It wasn't that she was deliberately forbearing to help him, just that it had all happened so quickly, but of course she didn't want to give up her seat while being afraid that she might do so, from the sort of instinct which if she found a penny on the floor of a bus made her hand it to the conductor.

But the old man, with gusty sighs, was getting to his feet.

"I can't tell what ye're saying," he wheezed, "but I'm gettin' along. Ye sit and look at the lady, ye do."

"Thank you," said Neil shortly. Joanna was more amused still to watch him scan the fret-work holes in the partition, the lazy turn of his body contrasting with the anxiety of his hidden face.

She said, taking off her sunglasses: "Good morning!"

The shock in his eyes disappeared as quickly as it came. He snapped: "Keep your voice down!"

The injustice of it made her want to raise her voice in high-pitched protest. She shrugged elaborately, but he had already turned away from her back to the wall. She was chagrined at the speed with which he had absorbed his surprise at her presence, and then dismissed it from his thoughts. But she supposed that in his job one had to deal with the situation as it was, never as one would like it to be. In fact at that moment, she was doing the same.

2

Neil ordered a half pint of draught bitter. Joanna pulled her hat further down over her eyes and lit a cigarette. She had intermittent views of Terry's serious face as he sat down opposite Vincent. Neil, leaning negligently into the corner of the settle, applied his ear physically to the nearest hole. Joanna did the same, and for a moment she felt herself straining into absolute silence, each old man in the public bar was a contemplative island, each had some liquid in the glass in front of him so that no conversation of any kind was taking place.

Terry's quiet voice was a shock into the stillness.

"Glad you made it."

She was aware of Vincent shifting in his seat.

"I had to talk to you."

"Good morning, Rose. Vincent?"

"Oh, a half."

"Right. Two halves, please, Rose."

"Right you are, Terry. Vincent."

There was a short pause.

"I had to talk to you."

"So you said. But you know already what I'll suggest."

"Terry—look, there were no letters, nothing to show for it." Joanna heard Terry's abrupt laugh.

"I mean," said Vincent quickly, "there's nothing, absolutely nothing . . ."

"I'm not thinking of that angle."

"Of what, then?"

"Of you I suppose." Joanna found herself listening for a note of tenderness in Terry's voice, but it sounded merely musing, objective. "You're not going to stand up to it. It's obvious a mile off that you're worried. It wouldn't need a good detecive to tell that *you're* hiding something, mate, and we've got a good detective in Carter, a bloody good one!"

Joanna shifted her gaze quickly to Neil Carter, but Terry's latest remark seemed to have had no personal impact on him. He was gazing down at his knees, frowning, concentrating everything of himself into the one faculty of hearing.

"I know it's getting me down . . ."

Terry's laugh, harsher. "The understatement of the year. And there's another thing . . ."

"What's that, for God's sake?"

There was a second pause. By shifting again Joanna could just see, until it moved out of sight, Terry's thoughtful face.

"The morality of truth, mate," said Terry at last, heavily. Neil's eyebrows rose and fell, without his moving anything else. "Which probably has a practical application as well in this instance," went on Terry. "If they clear your business out of the way, there'll be considerably less clutter, and more chance of finding out what happened. And they'll perhaps start looking at Julia a different way, which might begin to get them somewhere."

"There isn't a different way to start looking at Julia!" protested Vincent, and Joanna thought that Terry's laugh then was more cynical, more knowing, than she remembered ever having heard before, from Terry or from anyone else.

"Thank you," he said immediately afterwards, in a light tone which shocked her in its contrast, but a blur of movement through the holes showed that his and Vincent's drinking orders had arrived.

"Cheers, then," said Terry gravely.

"Cheers. Look, Terry," said Vincent on a gulp, "all right, if I do speak . . . I just don't know how to begin . . ."

"Oh, you won't have to, friend, you won't have to," said Neil Carter under his breath, making Joanna jump. He looked up for a moment and smiled at her, but he was really smiling into the path which was at least part of the way clear before him again.

"It'll come when you open your mouth," said Terry, "and you've only got to tell the truth. Vincent!" he said sharply.

"Yes?"

"You've told me the truth? You're sure you've told me the truth always? And by that I mean have you told me the whole truth, there's no part of it you've left out?"

"Terry," said Vincent, on an injured wail, "you *know* . . . all the way along I've told you and only you . . ."

"I know you've told me all the way along. It's the end, Julia's final and irremediable end, that I'm talking about now."

"I don't know anything about that. Terry, I swear it!" Joanna saw Vincent's profile again as he leaned forward. Then Vincent said, in a different tone, "You swear to me too, Terry, you swear. We all had the same opportunity."

She tried, and failed, to get a glimpse of Terry's face. His voice said quietly:

"Quite right, Vincent. And I swear to you. I swear that I know nothing of Julia's death."

There was another, the longest, pause, then glasses hit back at the table.

"You think I should talk to that detective, then?"

"I reckon it's the only thing you can do."

"You may get into trouble too," said Vincent, "unless I can keep back that I told you, for suppressing possible evidence."

"I'll ride that. It will be the best thing," said Terry dreamily, "to tell the truth."

Joanna had a strange feeling that Terry had in some way found his conversation with Vincent upsetting, that it had started trains of thought which he found unwelcome.

Vincent had undoubtedly benefited from it. His pale blue jacket shot across the space beside Joanna, from shoulder to pocket, descending again as he spoke.

"Thanks, Terry, I know you're right. I suppose I knew it all the time, really."

"I suppose you did."

"I'll get in touch with that detective."

"You do that, Vincent." Terry still sounded preoccupied.

"I will."

"You better go now, anyway. I'll follow on."

"Thanks."

"I didn't do anything," said Terry heavily.

Coins clinked on the table and Vincent's body rose past the spaces. Terry, Neil and Joanna sat on in silence punctuated by glasses being lifted and set down. Neil Carter looked at his watch once, and grimaced. Wriggle as she would, Joanna couldn't manage to catch sight of Terry. It was a long ten minutes before he rose on an audible sigh and walked away. Neil waited another two minutes or so before speaking and Joanna, patient in her absorption and curiosity, waited for Neil. He surprised her. Showing her the points of his canine teeth he leaned over the table.

"You extraordinary, fascinating woman! You told me just so much, didn't you?"

He hadn't, after all, dismissed what she had done, he had merely put it aside until a convenient moment.

"I needn't have bothered being so clever," she said.

"You should have known me well enough by now," said Neil, ever so slightly injured, "to know that I would have acquainted myself with everything about everybody in *Summer Time* which could possibly be classified as a habit."

"I should have done," she conceded humbly.

The atmosphere was friendly, mutually respectful, as she most liked it to be with Neil Carter.

"What are you going to do?" she asked him, taking a chance that there would be no more snubs.

"I thought I was going to seek him out, and so I shall if he fails to seek me. But after leaving in such a flurry of resolve . . . well, I'll leave him the initiative."

"I'll be surprised if he doesn't take it, he's been in agony. But—what's the secret he shared with the fair Julia?"

She felt very happy, and smiled unstintingly at Neil Carter.

"Have a proper drink," suggested Neil.

"I'll have a dry martini. Plain." That was what she had had with Terry. Terry whose heaviness of heart was not to do with any guilty complicity in the death of Julia. Oh, it wasn't, he had sworn. "But—wouldn't it be wiser to go our ways?"

"None of them ever comes into the Public," said Neil categorically.

"Having just seen what you made of the limited information I gave you, I believe you! About Julia and Vincent," she said again, when the drinks had arrived.

"I hate to admit that your guess is as good as mine. I hate to be baffled!"

"Yet you choose a job in which something you hate must be a regular occupational hazard?"

"So it seems. But when I solve the puzzle it's All Worth While. I've got to solve this one, Joanna!"

"Because?"

"Because it's so apparently *in*soluble. And because—it will influence my future."

"I thought so, somehow. I'm sorry I was so meanly selective with the help I gave you. I won't be like that again."

"I know you won't. Keep looking and listening. And thanks at least for letting me know promptly enough this morning. See you Saturday, and probably before then, in the hotel or the theatre."

She thought a gleam came into his eye. He probably enjoyed the deceit of pretending they were strangers—which was more than she did, the cold encounters made her feel uncomfortable and disloyal in all directions.

"I'll go first," said Neil, "because I'm late for an appointment. If you should be unlucky enough to be spotted coming out of the Public, you bought cigarettes."

She had already worked out the alibi, but she thought he now meant well by her for most of the time, and so she thanked him, without comment, for his suggestion. She still saw, as she had seen at the beginning, that he was ruthless and ambitious and capable of being cruel, but between her and him the aggression was dying down.

3

Joanna walked slowly back to *Seaview*, wearing the sunglasses because of the dazzle but swinging the hat from her hand. It was lovely not to feel furtive, lovely to feel stronger and less afraid of the past, remembered or forgotten.

There was a hubbub in the hall of the hotel. The centre of it was a tall thin unfamiliar figure, strikingly attractive with a lined boyish face, dressed with exquisite casualness. She had forgotten Geoffrey was coming, and remembered as she saw that Clare was standing closer to the newcomer than anyone else and that her normally pale and serious face was pink and faintly smiling. Joanna also noticed that Vincent was almost sustaining a euphoric smile, and that when it slipped it gave way to an expression of great sternness and resolve for which Vincent had to work on unsuitable features. It could well be that he was actually thinking Stiff Upper Lip, in so many words.

Geoffrey's eyes fell on Joanna, and stayed there in gentle inquiry. Clare put out a hand to her.

"This is Joanna."

Gail hastened forward to explain. Joanna's immediate impression of Geoffrey's warmth and kindness was strengthened, because he spent several moments out of his precious few hours in Linton talking to her as if there was nobody else. The rest of them, even Clare, withdrew a little, as if to allow her the full occasion of meeting their producer.

"They need me just now, rather more than my other companies," he told her lightly and quietly. "But I've only so much time to give them. That's the worst of being overextended, you haven't got the extra time when it's unexpectedly needed. But I love work so much I've forgotten how to use leisure."

"You're so lucky." Joanna had to smile at his bright intelligent face. "Now, please don't give me any more of your working time. Except just to hear me say how much I enjoyed the show."

"They're a great company, aren't they?" said Geoffrey, looking even brighter, then swiftly sad.

"They're great off stage as well as on. I'm so terribly sorry . . ."

As she moved away she saw Terry, and knew with a pang that he was worried. She watched him, and it was only with an effort that he was in touch with his surroundings, even with the red-letter fact of Geoffrey's arrival.

It will be the best thing to tell the truth.

Joanna recalled the tone in which the disembodied Terry had said those words, and she was now certain the conversation which had done so much for Vincent had sunk Terry in a profound disquiet.

CHAPTER 13

I

Lunch was even more animated than usual. Joanna sensed a sort of relief in the gaiety, as if everyone in the cast of *Summer Time* was glad to be able to look at somebody beside Gail and herself without suspicion. She noticed that when they weren't looking at their plates they were looking at Geoffrey, for whom room had been made in the centre of the room beside Clare. He was that kind of person, of course, and they had needed him. Only Terry, under Joanna's steady scrutiny, was still not giving himself wholeheartedly to the event of Geoffrey's visit, there were long moments in which he gazed expressionlessly into space. Gail even roused him a couple of times and Joanna saw something which frightened her in the split second between his unheeding abstraction and the radiant smile he turned upon her. But he had sworn to Vincent that he was not concerned in Julia's death.

But somebody was.

It was, after all, hard to decide whose smile was the more fearsome, Mrs. Berkeley's or Mrs. Tompkins'. Joanna admired the way Geoffrey side-stepped both ladies as he left the dining-room and ended up on a lounge sofa wedged between Clare and Rhoda and flanked by Arthur and Terry. Ma Tompkins gave up and retired to the office but Mrs. Berkeley came into the lounge and sat by Joanna, making no attempt to disguise the fact that she was interested solely in the conversation of which Geoffrey was the centre and that she was straining to hear it. She had a curious habit of murmuring an acknowledgement of the remarks made across the room, and jerked continuously in her seat. Sandra, Susie and Sonia seemed to be paying less deference to their mother than they normally did, draping themselves round chair backs and over chair arms in the vicinity of

Geoffrey without their usual frequent glances across to her. Joanna guessed that Geoffrey had once expressed a dislike of her hegemony, and that when he was around she did her best to moderate its outward show, while her daughters took advantage.

Geoffrey drained his coffee cup and looked at his watch. He took hold of Clare's hand and held it to his side while he whispered in her ear. She nodded, biting her lip as if to try and contain the happiness escaping into her face. He got up.

"I'm going to my little room under the eaves." His soft voice filled the room. Joanna remembered that he was a player as well as a producer. "We'll meet together in the theatre at five. Now—if any of you want a private chat with me during the afternoon, I'll be upstairs. I'll hang out Mrs. Tompkins' 'Do not disturb' sign if I'm in conference."

There was a sudden stillness. Geoffrey smiled round on them all a bit painfully and strode out of the room. The stillness hung on, and Joanna thought the eyes were at last almost nakedly wary. Clare bit her lip a second time against her inappropriate happiness.

"Is this the first time Geoffrey's been here since Julia's death?" Joanna spoke very quietly to Mrs. Berkeley.

"Second," said Mrs. Berkeley shortly, continuing her avid sweep of the room and not even glancing towards Joanna. Joanna followed her gaze, and they were the only two who were not sitting motionless, waiting for someone to leave the room and have it thought he or she had something to unburden to Geoffrey. It was eventually Terry who rose, watched in silence as he went out. If only it had been Vincent! But Vincent was now geared for the real confrontation and had no need of Geoffrey. He was sitting looking down at the floor, his mouth for the moment relaxed, but he jumped with the rest of them when Gail said, loudly and triumphantly:

"There goes Terry for his walk!"

Joanna swivelled round just in time to see the yellow head moving down the path.

Arthur got up then. He held on to the back of a chair and talked to them. With his paper-white face and plastic teeth and short neat hair he looked so unreal Joanna wondered if that was the reason he had animals in his act rather than dolls. He said that if anyone thought he or she might feel better for a talk with Geoffrey, then he or she should go upstairs. They were fortunate to have someone so gifted and so kind as Geoffrey to be concerned with them, and for his sake at least, if they had nothing to say to him, they should try not to think about what had happened to Julia because it would do no good and would merely serve to deepen the sense of mistrust which was growing up between them.

"This mystery," said Arthur wearily, "may well never be solved. And so we should not continue to feel suspicious of one another. The person concerned—he or she—will know. The rest—should not penalise or be penalised."

"Thanks, Arthur," said Rhoda. She got up and stood over him and leaned down to kiss his white cheek. "You're right, as usual."

She glared challengingly round on them, then sauntered out. Arthur sat down again. Vincent leaned across to Thelma and tenderly took her hand, and at almost the same second Dirk leaned across to Delia and did the same thing. Joanna had difficulty not laughing, and she caught Robbie's eye above the fingers she spread over her twitching mouth. He winked at her.

She would like to have left the room but it was her clear duty to wait and see what everybody else did, and to tell Neil Carter whether they stayed in the lounge, or went upstairs following Geoffrey's invitation. It was the sort of job that young constables sighed heavily over in TV series.

But it turned out to be no job at all. Everybody was so anxious to end this particular scene that the lounge was clear in fifteen minutes and everyone, fired perhaps by Rhoda's spirit, went upstairs. Gail in the end was the only one left, and looked downcast when Joanna said she was going upstairs too.

"Why don't *you* go and talk to Geoffrey?" suggested Joanna. "You're the one person who can do that without anything being thought about it. And—I should think you'd be glad to talk to the other person who wasn't there—that night."

Gail nodded, absently and glumly. Her bare brown leg moved to and fro where she balanced on the chair arm across the room, coral toenails just showing through the mouth of the minimal sandal which hung and swung an inch from the floor.

"What's the matter?"

"Nothing with me," said Gail to the ground. "But I think something's up with Terry." All at once she was looking with entreaty at Joanna. "Don't you think something's up with him?"

"I don't know him well enough."

"You may not have known him long," said Gail, re-examining the precariously balancing sandal, "but you've seen pretty much of him since you came . . . I mean, did he seem—worried—when he brought you back last night?" Joanna thought this was the first time Gail had asked her a question without looking at her.

"I wasn't in a condition to notice, really, but I thought he was reasonably cheerful. Better than he is today, perhaps. But you've got to remember that everybody's—a bit touchy at the moment. You told me so yourself."

"I know, I know. But I still feel there's something more with Terry . . ."

She raised her head again and they stared at each other. Joanna found herself reflecting what a nice person Gail was.

"Is Terry married?"

She really wondered, for a second, whether she had said it or thought it, she had thought it so often.

Gail showed her astonishment.

"Don't you know?"

"I have no idea. Those jokes on the stage . . ."

"All comedians make those, except the ones who are obviously . . . Terry's wife died last year."

The dark woman in the photograph.

"Oh, poor Terry!" But she had to hide her pleasure that he had had a wife.

"Yes. She was killed in a car crash. He wasn't involved. He wasn't there. It must be awful, that," said Gail, "sudden silence for ever after. I mean, think if you'd quarrelled . . ."

"Yes . . ." Oh, God, it must be awful, awful. Poor Terry. Poor world, in which such things could happen. Sudden silence for ever after. Poor, poor . . . Her body was made of rubber, that was why she hardly felt the sharp corners on the way down. She smiled up at Gail.

"Oh, Gail," she said, holding out her hand.

Gail took it. Gail was kneeling down. That was a strange thing, but when she, Joanna, turned her head, it rasped against something rough and when she tried to lean forward she couldn't do it. Gail had turned to speak to someone just out of Joanna's sight and when she turned back again she had a glass of water in her hand.

"Oh, no!" said Joanna in disgust, knowing what had happened. She was lying on the floor, and there would be bruises later on her thigh and an elbow, although at the moment she was quite comfortable. Gail put her arm under Joanna's head and lifted it up, then expertly gave her some water. There were freckles on Gail's bare brown arm and her scent was powerful but friendly.

"Better?"

"Yes. Yes."

Miss Waterhouse moved round into view and her anxious face made Joanna better still, and too irritated any longer to be comfortable. She struggled to sit up and managed it with their help. Then, less easily, to her feet.

She held on to the back of a chair. She was better every second.

"Don't you think you should see a doctor?" suggested Miss Waterhouse fussily.

"It's only nerves," said Joanna. "Nerves and low blood pressure."

She knew there was nothing physically wrong with her, just congenital low blood pressure and mental pressure reaching out from the murk at her back . . . But she wasn't interested in her own mystery, the more she could forget it the better she would be. This was for sure, because she suddenly remembered that these dizzy spells had been happening at home, before she had decided she could no longer cope. They had been happening far more frequently than they were happening now. It was strange that she should have forgotten.

"Please don't tell anyone else," she asked the two women, "it's nothing and it's getting less."

She smiled from one to the other of them. She was all right again, and demonstrated it by walking ahead of them. "Please," she said.

"So long as you'll go and lie down for a while," said Gail. Miss Waterhouse clicked her tongue, but said nothing.

"I like the idea of it," said Joanna.

They hovered while she walked upstairs. The world through the Window was softer-coloured than it had been the afternoon of her arrival. The room was deeply familiar. Joanna got quickly into bed and fell asleep.

2

She thought the knocking on the door coincided with her own natural process of awakening, it wasn't a shock, it was a friendly marking of the transition. In answer to her lazy summons Miss Waterhouse came in with a tray, making heavy weather of negotiating the door. There was a meal on it, and Miss Waterhouse looked anxiously from the slightly slopped soup to Joanna. Joanna sat up, feeling the cheerfulness of her smile and seeing it reflected in the relief of Miss Waterhouse's.

"You're feeling better!"

"I'm feeling wonderful, I've been asleep for— What time is it?"

"Seven. We thought we'd leave you as long as possible." Miss Waterhouse put the tray across Joanna's knees, spilling more soup.

"You're awfully good." Dinner was normally at half past six. It was the only disadvantage to *Seaview.*

Miss Waterhouse left, sooner than she would have done if Joanna hadn't been unencouraging. The gravy coverlet to the meat and vegetables was only slightly set, and Joanna ate everything on the tray with an appetite. Then she lay back again, looking out on the flushed sky and feeling unusually clear-minded. This was the time to start thinking systematically and analytically about Julia's possible murderers, even perhaps to write a few thoughts down in an attempt to clarify them. She would take everyone in turn.

Rhoda. *There is nothing in anything I've seen, or been told, to connect Rhoda in any way with Julia's death.*

Clare. *In it for Geoffrey, and has got him. Did Julia's death remove an obstacle?*

Susie, Sonia and Sandra. *Just can't differentiate between them . . .*

Someone was whistling on the promenade below the open window. The hotel was very quiet and when the whistling had passed by the whole world was quiet, with the distant regular pulse of silence.

The silence was broken by another knock on the door, and this time Joanna woke up with a jerk. It was dark, and the street lamp outside weakly illumined Miss Waterhouse's face in the doorway, the electric light on the landing behind her sharply outlined her untidy hair and cardigan-clad shoulders.

"Mrs. Stuart . . ."

"I'm all right, just got sleeping sickness, it seems."

She was still half sitting up, in the position in which she had begun her survey of the murder, and she reached out her hand and switched the lamp on. It was half-past ten. Miss Waterhouse seemed unappeased.

"Mrs. Stuart, Miss Chapman is on the telephone for you."

Wary, her heart racing, which of her committee women was that? She couldn't remember and she didn't want to.

"Miss Chapman?"

"From the theatre. Clare," said Miss Waterhouse selfconsciously.

"Oh, Clare!"

Joanna got out of bed carefully, briefly dizzy again in her relief. She pulled her dressing-gown on and went downstairs after the retreating Miss Waterhouse. Clare had rung the call box.

"Forgive me for coming on at this extraordinary time." Joanna hardly recognised Clare's voice, it was so lively. There were also lively background noises.

"I'd expected you all back any moment."

"Yes, but we're having a party and I want you to come. Joanna, I'm going to marry Geoffrey."

"Clare!"

"We got engaged in the interval, too late for me to ring you then. Could you come along right away and have a drink with us?"

"Could I!"

That was as good as any moment she could recall, standing in the small space and reading the list of telephone exchange codes a few inches from her nose, smelling floor polish and learning that Clare had thought of her at such a time.

"Terry's dressing-room," said Clare, "and come in by the stage door of course."

3

She was there in twenty minutes. Fred of the stage door locked it after her and accompanied her to the party, which he made a point of telling her he had left in order to be around to let her in. Terry's dressing-room was very warm and smoky and seemed to be packed with people, but she and Fred and a couple of stage staff and the musicians Jake and Charlie were the only people there beside the players. From the doorway Joanna found Terry and then Clare, and went up to Clare and kissed her, in gratitude as well as congratulation. Geoffrey was there at once with a glass of champagne.

"Even this, you see," he said to Joanna, "I fitted into the schedule."

"I see. And no doubt you will get married in it, too."

"Well, in a scheduled break." He smiled at her. At least when he paused for conversation, he gave it all his attention. He seemed the sort of man who would give all his attention to whatever he was doing.

"When?" she asked him.

"Just before Christmas."

And Clare will give up the stage, thought Joanna, pretty double quick. Perhaps do a little high class modelling. Head and shoulders . . .

Terry's arm was across her shoulders. It was extraordinary how many identical gestures were differently informed. Dirk's bow and Arthur's. Delia's use of the word *madame* and Arthur's use of it. Terry's arm on her shoulders, and Neil Carter's . . .

"I'm glad you came," said Terry.

"I'm glad *you're* glad." Emphasising the word "you're" made the silly phrase sincere. She wanted him to know she was glad. There was a sense of occasion, she thought, in the grave way they looked at one another. Something took place in it. Not the first thing that had taken place between her and Terry. A sort of shifting into a position of greater comfort. So many shifts, in so few days! Now, after this latest one, she was able to lean beyond him and pick up the photograph from the dressing-table.

"This is your wife, Terry?"

"It is."

"I'm sorry."

He was smiling and grave at the same time. "Thank you."

"Gail tells me," said Joanna, replacing the photograph, thinking more of the sad look of it—by association?—than of what she was saying, "that all comedians except the queer ones have statutory wives to tell jokes against."

"That's right." Terry gave his snort of a laugh. "The night Myra died—when I'd just heard about it and hadn't been there—I had to go on and tell jokes against her."

"Terry!"

He smiled, laid his finger against her cheek. "Don't be shocked. Don't be sad. It didn't make any difference."

"I know that. I'm just thinking about hundreds of people idly laughing."

"And they had better be! When you said that show business took no account of trends and politics, you left out the other big thing."

"Which is?" She was ridiculously pleased that he had memorised her remark.

"The personality of the individual, how he or she feels. It takes no account of that. Some people can't keep it going. The suicide rate among comedians is comparatively high."

He sounded impersonal, even flippant, but how long and deep had his own struggle been? Joanna didn't think many people would know.

Gail was there, setting her drink down rather carefully on the dressing-table beside the photograph and putting an arm round him and an arm round Joanna. She looked at Terry first, briefly, then keenly at Joanna. She said nothing about the scene in the lounge until Terry had moved away, summoned by Geoffrey.

"How are you?" asked Gail then, accusingly.

"I'm fine. It was good of you not to let on."

Gail shrugged. "You asked me not to."

It was hard to believe Gail had so lately dragged costumes on and off, had her hair scraped back while she covered her face with cold cream. Her coiffure held its usual elaborate large outline, symmetrically softened with the ever-crisp tendrils. Her skin was fine natural bronze, lightly freckled over the nose when one got close, her large brown eyes were subtly emphasised, her beautiful body just evident inside a featureless emerald silk sheath. Sometimes Joanna thought she saw in Gail's eyes, when they followed Terry, a kind of helpless amazement that he did not love her, because who could do more than she did, to be lovely and to love? And yet it was clear that Gail knew she was not loved, which was realism. How complicated people were, how inconsistent! And here were she and Neil trying to solve a murder mystery which had so many complicated, inconsistent suspects, trained to dissemble at a possible cost to their very selves, and no clues.

Joanna emptied her glass and Robbie immediately filled it again for her. He stayed and talked to her for a while and it was absurd, for a start, to suspect *him,* with his honest eyes and quiet manner and apparently small amiable ego. *Apparently.* Joanna, feeling happiness expanding in her head with the fumes of the champagne, had to force herself to look critically and analytically at Robbie while, spurred by her automatic short questions, he talked about the ways of his Highland youth. Even while she wasn't really listening to the sense of his words she was regretting that she wasn't. Robbie wasn't a bore like some of them, but there might be clues if she was alert enough to pick them up.

Joanna let Arthur fill her glass for the third time. She raised it, responding to Rhoda's toast across the room. She had once read a murder mystery whose last chapter had been removed by a library joker. This one could turn out the same, and there would be no getting hold of another copy.

"You are pensive, madame," remarked Arthur.

She smiled at him in her relief as he touched her cheek. Different from Terry! His obtrusive hands were in fact rather small and neat, not unlike Terry's, but they were more beautifully manicured, smoother, whiter-backed . . . One pair of *Summer Time* hands had gone round Julia's throat and pressed and squeezed until she was dead. That was *for certain.* Joanna looked round on the flushed, happy faces.

"I was just thinking of contrasts, Arthur. Such sadness. Now all at once, such joy."

"The *chiaroscuro* of life," said Arthur, rather absently and probably not for the first time. "The dark illumines the light."

"But *such* dark . . ."

He patted her arm and moved on. Joanna looked round her as well as she could. Fred and the stage staff were just slipping out. Mrs. Berkeley was making a disproportionate disturbance in a corner, trying to round up her girls. There must have been three stage people present at one point, because Brian was haranguing one, leaning against the wall and speaking very quickly and without expression in his face. Delia was talking gratingly near Joanna's ear to Vincent about Vienna. Vincent was exaggerating his real interest,

Joanna was sure, smiling and encouraging and then, in Delia's longest monologue, jutting his chin and firming his mouth, acting out his new resolution. It was clear that nothing had happened since she had looked at him after lunch and she hoped he would go to Neil before Neil came to him, Neil wouldn't give him much more time. She was surprised that Pam still looked so calmly pleased with herself. Why hadn't Neil asked her what she had finally forborne to tell Joanna? As a sop to her working role Joanna edged up to Pam and asked her, very quietly into her ear, if she was still sure she didn't want to talk about anything.

There was a reaction, which Joanna's fourth glass of champagne perhaps made her exaggerate. Pam looked round the room quickly and furtively as Joanna asked her question, relaxing only when she saw—what? Joanna tried to follow Pam's restored little smile, but it could have been covering half the room. Pam said, politely but very firmly:

"Quite sure, thank you, Mrs. Stuart. I had been going to ask your advice but then the problem solved itself. That often happens when you decide to do something, don't you find?"

"I hadn't thought."

Pam's flat words, flatly uttered, had been accompanied by an uncharacteristic widening of her smile and ended in a trill of laughter —which from across the room would have made it seem that she was talking anything but mysteries, would have lulled the suspicions of anyone who might have been thinking that Pam . . . Was Pam afraid of someone?

"This is no time for intellectual effort," said Brenda softly beside her.

"No occasion is, so far as I'm concerned," said Joanna. Brenda could just give one an inferiority complex, not because she had an honours degree in history from Cambridge, not from flaunting her exceptional qualities, she did everything quietly, but from not being quite able to hide them. She was always alone somehow, and she was alone now, Joanna had seen her stalking the room with her glass, pausing to chat but as if never losing sight of her objective. Had she reached her objective now, reaching Joanna?

"You want to solve our mystery, though, don't you?" suggested Brenda, faintly smiling.

"What makes you think I want to do that?"

But if anyone had seen her with Detective Inspector Carter she would as soon it was Brenda, who would be the least inclined to be shocked.

"For no reason I can define. Perhaps from one or two small things you've said, how you've looked."

"Can you help me, then?"

"I shouldn't think so. I might correct a few impressions."

"Such as?"

Friendly faces blurred past, but she declined to meet their eyes. She must keep Brenda going. It could be that even Brenda, amid so much champagne and good will, was behaving with a rare indiscretion.

"The impressions you have doubtless universally received of the lady herself."

Joanna started to say "J-u-l-i-a" on an incredulous note, then bit it off. The one word would be enough to turn every head, kill every piece of conversation.

"Everyone said how super she was."

"Oh, she was," said Brenda, "and super clever too, which was perhaps less well realised. Because she was a complete phoney."

"Phoney? But I've read reviews, heard people talking . . ."

"Oh, I don't mean her act." Brenda was never impatient, angry, upset, she was always alertly indifferent, but sometimes other reactions could be sensed. "I mean *her*. The warmth, the spontaneity, it was all immensely careful."

"How do you know?"

Cold glittered for a second in Brenda's eyes. Joanna thought, she doesn't like to be questioned.

"I do. Oh, I can't give you *evidence*, anything like that, for goodness' sake! But you can take my word for it. Julia was a brilliant fake."

"Do you think anybody shares your perception?"

The cold had given way to an approving amusement. Brenda shrugged.

"I don't think so, unless they're as big hypocrites as I am."

"So you appeared to go along with the consensus?"

She shrugged again. "Why not? It was what Julia—and everyone else—liked to hear. I had no quarrel with Julia."

Hadn't she? Brenda was surely Neil Carter's most formidable challenge.

"The bride and groom are leaving," observed Brenda.

Geoffrey was balanced gracefully on a small table near the door. He thanked them all for their energy and their courage, wished them luck for the last three weeks of the season.

"I'll be with you on your last night. You all know where you can reach me—or you can add something to Clare's undiplomatic bag."

Clare stood beside the table leaning against Geoffrey's knee, dreaming into space. "You're all invited to the wedding, by the way," said Geoffrey, "which includes Joanna. Written confirmation to follow."

He blew a kiss and jumped down, and left the room with Clare. The euphoria went with them. Everyone immediately set to tidying up, moving quietly about the room and out into the corridor with ashtrays and empty bottles, saying only essential things. Joanna came across Delia in tears in a corner, ostensibly groping for cigarette ends, and when she tried to be comforting she received only an incoherent mittel-European response. Delia's behaviour could be simply a reaction to too much champagne or the sight of Clare's happiness. In the circumstances, Clare's happiness had brought a lump to Joanna's throat, too. Delia was a simple, romantic soul. Or so it seemed.

CHAPTER 14

I

Rhoda. *There's nothing in anything I've seen, or heard, to connect Rhoda with Julia's death. But equally, nothing to make such a connexion impossible. She's unusually strong, I should say, mentally as well as physically, that lazy steady way of moving could indicate exceptional purpose and self-discipline.*

Clare. *The most transparent and straightforward of the females,* I think. *In it for Geoffrey, and has got him. As with Rhoda, nothing I know to connect her with the murder, but did Julia's death remove an obstacle? Neil will have an idea about that.*

Pam. *As above, except that she almost did something which was surely out of character. I should think she's hard as nails. Neil must have got hold of her by now and she hasn't turned a hair.*

Brenda. *Formidable, and if Julia really was somebody to be seen through, Brenda saw. She would be ruthless if she thought it was necessary, no doubt of that. Perhaps Julia attacked her, and she . . . No, strangling could never be an act of self-defence. This is all conjecture. As above, there's nothing I know to connect Brenda with the murder. Except perhaps . . . I get a feeling sometimes, which I've nothing to support, that Brenda isn't interested in men.*

Susie, Sonia and Sandra. *Just can't differentiate between them. Can only assume that what's good for one is good for the others. Or bad. Susie hates her mother. Hatred is hatred. All three girls must be terribly repressed, Julia wasn't repressed at all, she could do anything, and perhaps did. All this is* conjecture.

Mrs. Berkeley. *Well, I should like it to be Mrs. Berkeley, as it has to be someone, but can't see it. Unless, of course, Julia threatened one of the girls in some way, even unknowingly. And Mrs. Berkeley is obsessive in one direction, why not in others? But there's nothing I've seen or heard, etc.*

Brian. *His passions are stated: politics and music. Julia I suppose could have offended against either, and I should say his political passions are the wrong side of fanatical. And, as above, if obsessed in one direction, why not in others? This is impossible. Poor Neil.*

Robbie. *Nothing whatever to say here. Seems so normal, so good-natured.*

Vincent. *Self-confessed connexion which must at least look fishy or he wouldn't have been so hung up. Homosexual, which lays open to blackmail. Hard to see how this could fit, but Neil may tell me. Seems anxious to tell the truth, but there are double bluffs.*

Thelma. *If Julia is phoney, so is Thelma. Can't imagine her feeling deeply enough to take drastic action, but with such a type self-regard could be a terrific spur. Shouldn't write like this, there's nothing, etc. etc.*

Arthur. *Absorbed in his vocation, apparently no longer interested in women. Apparently, apparently, everything's apparently. But Julia was a pro, too, and Arthur appreciated that. He was affected, despite himself, when he spoke of her death to me on the beach.*

Delia. *Emotional, obviously. Unimaginative, I suspect. Which combination could perhaps produce the temperament of someone who would commit murder. Sunday night she was distraught for no apparent reason. But there's nothing etc. etc.*

Dirk. *The drive behind his and his sister's ordered lives. If something threatened to disturb this order? But apparently there's nothing.*

Terry. *The only one besides Vincent who's obviously worried. Oh, they're all subdued and upset, of course, but Terry's worried, he's got something on his mind, on his conscience by the recent look of him. He was the confidanto of Vincent's secret. Why? He was married but that doesn't cut out the other.*

Joanna picked up her pen, and after a long look towards the elusive horizon, bent her head reluctantly again over the notepad.

Four days further on. I've been in a privileged position here now for over a week. Where has it got me? Absolutely nowhere. I think despite Arthur's plea the tension's getting worse. Pam's still unruffled, which even for her is superhuman. Neil Carter must have tackled her. Terry looks sicker and sicker. And Vincent is all sort of exhausted and purged. Having talked to him, Neil Carter will be ahead of me again. I must have seemed the biggest break he could have had, but I'm not doing anything about it . . .

There was a knock on the door. Thelma called, liltingly sweet, "We're just off, Joanna!" and she called back that she was coming, throwing her pen down in relief. The exercise was disturbing as well as futile.

Joanna had been glad to discover that there was somebody or other playing tennis every morning, and within two or three days it had become known that she could always be relied on to make up a set. Within two or three days, too, she felt as if her routine at *Seaview* had been going on for ever. Tennis in the morning; what she called to herself a cabaret lunch; a walk in the afternoon into town or behind the town or the other way among the dunes; a swim, sometimes in company; a solitary dinner, maybe flanked by some stilted conversation with Mrs. Tompkins and/or Miss Waterhouse; another, shorter, walk afterwards; and finally reading until they all poured back in from the theatre, good for at least a couple of rueful anecdotes and perhaps tired enough—one of them—to let something slip, although when Friday came round again she was still waiting for this. On Friday night she would be coming home with them—Terry had given her another ticket for the show.

On Friday, too, the distraction of tennis was especially welcome. A letter had arrived from Daphne, and the fact of it had been so crushing she had gone upstairs after breakfast like an old woman. She didn't open the letter until she was in her room, sitting in the Window, and after looking a long time across the sea. Daphne thought the set-up was all very odd, and she must say she was surprised that Joanna hadn't found time to telephone before setting off for the seaside. It was surely time to start looking round for a nursing-home for the old aunt, the present arrangements being so unsatisfactory, and she appended a list of suitable establishments in the Linton area. Joanna was only thankful that Daphne didn't ask her how Peter was supposed to fit into her arrangements, and tell her off for putting her husband second to her aunt—even though he was away. It was an uncharacteristic oversight on Daphne's part, but she was grateful for it. Another solace was that Daphne did not intend to come to Linton (as Joanna, noting her relief, had feared she might), unless Joanna asked her to.

She had picked up her analysis of Tivoli suspects and attempted to add to it in an effort to shut out Daphne and the alarm bells she had started ringing, but during the tennis she suddenly saw there was no reason for her to do what Daphne thought best for her, no need to consider Daphne's feelings so far as her own life was concerned. It was more a revelation than a realisation and made her lose her awareness of the game, so that the service she was waiting to receive struck her in the chest, producing an appropriate temporary breathlessness. Joanna wrote back to Daphne after lunch, thanking her for her concern, telling her the aunt situation was already under control and that after it had been wound up she intended to stay on in Linton for a holiday. *But don't dream of coming down. At the moment I'm very busy and crowded, and when I've finished I shall want to be idle and solitary. I'll let you know in due course my precise plans.*

Sitting in the Window and sealing the envelope, Joanna was aware that she had surprised herself once again, because she had changed so much. Yet everything was following from the same change, the putting of herself into the centre of her life, for the first time that she could remember. Selfishness was now motivating all her actions, and yet she had never felt less self-absorbed, more truly concerned with other people.

It was wonderful to be waiting again for the Tivoli curtain to rise, to be swamped again by the *fortissimo* of the organ and drums. The woman beside her was not the same woman she had sat by the Friday before, but they exchanged the same smile of shared anticipation. Joanna couldn't be certain that Terry told all new jokes, but she didn't recognise anything in the show except the start and the finish and the succession of moods and players and talents. Terry was an expectant father (Joanna hoped with a pang that he had a child) and Brian a severe doctor. There was a sustained skit on a popular television quiz show. Arthur opposed his long-suffering feline with a sleek white rabbit which at the end of his act was suddenly alive, wrinkling a pink nose and running away across the table while Arthur exhibited two empty hands. The rabbit disappeared under the curtain, and Arthur's rabbit voice petered out in a muffled squeak—Joanna suspected the disappearance was unscheduled and Arthur's reaction a brilliant *ad lib,* and there was a noticeable increase in rapport between players and audience. Terry as a milkman kept trying to get to grips with Gail as a housewife, always frustrated by the recurring return of husband Robbie and offering ever wider explanations of his continued presence and ambiguous postures. The central musical scene was an Al Jolson medley, which gave scope for comic business as well as singing and dancing. And when they sang and danced, how happy and carefree they looked! Joanna caught nobody off guard, at any point.

Brenda, the one for whom success on the stage probably meant least, was electrifying. The Berkeleys, Robbie, Dirk and Delia—the same but different. Joanna thought there was a new edge of mastery to Vincent's performance, that he just dominated an act which the week before he had shared as equal partner, and that it suited both him and Thelma, who was so deliciously, so graciously, feminine. Which came first with Thelma, the act or the life? Joanna couldn't imagine Thelma doing anything unstudied, certainly it was of all things macabre to imagine her hands tightening in the sudden brutal decisive gesture which had been necessary to kill Julia.

2

They still played to her, but tonight Terry gave his rose to a pretty girl of about fourteen on the other side of the auditorium. Joanna still went through the door that so totally divided the active and passive lives of the theatre, and expectantly along the warm corridors. Again she looked in on the girls and congratulated them, she even, on an impulse of curiosity, put her head round at the Berkeleys and Delia, and got the impression of a space between the two older women over which drifted the three tall pale girls like Rosetti damozels. Then she went to Terry's door and knocked, and when he answered from across the room she went gaily in and perched on the arm of the sofa so that he could see her each time he looked up from the mirror. He was cleaning his face but the orange make-up still smeared the yellow edge of his hair. His hand must have trembled when he applied it, she thought it was trembling now, as he wielded cotton wool. Also that something had happened to him not unlike what had happened to Vincent. As if a load had gone. His eyes sparkled as he looked towards her, the radiance of his smile was spontaneous again.

"You weren't bored a second time?"

"Bored? It was tremendous."

Her heart leapt to meet his mood. Not for the first time she had this childish, impetuous desire to make boisterous contact with him, to include him in her surge of joy at being alive, ruffle his hair, nudge her head against his cheek, take his hand. The impulse was so bizarre she found herself smiling.

"Why are you smiling?"

"I'm happy, I suppose."

"You look so much better," said Terry, "than when you arrived in Linton."

He had got up and held out his hands. Eagerly she got up too, and found that she had flung her arms round his neck. She kept them there, her face against his, for the brief moment in which he hugged her, then drew back, laughing in surprise and slight embarrassment. "You're a kind man," she said, as lightly as possible.

They were holding hands at arms' length, and she thought Terry was looking at her in a sort of amazement. It felt like a long, static silence before the door opened and they both turned their heads. It was only after she had seen it was Neil Carter that Joanna took her hands away. She said "Good evening" composedly to Neil (which even afterwards, thinking about it in bed, she didn't think she could have bettered), and Terry said, amiably so that his words made Joanna flinch, at least:

"I thought even policemen knocked on doors in Britain."

"I did knock, sir," said Neil apologetically, showing no reaction, but showing Joanna another side to his work which he must hate even more than being unable to solve puzzles: the having, so much of the time, to be deferential. She wondered how thoroughly he made up for it, when the opportunities came. "There was some noise in the corridor, which I'm afraid must have drowned it."

There still was, behind Neil, an ugly noise. The voice of Mrs. Berkeley chastising one or more of her daughters.

"Did you want something?" asked Terry.

"If it's not inconvenient, sir," said this incredibly compliant Neil, whose very features seemed to have softened, "I should like a further word with you."

He stood, the embodiment of patience, while Terry considered, and Joanna swallowed uncomfortably on the word *further*.

"All right," said Terry shortly, at last, and Joanna went back to the girls.

When they were all leaving, twenty minutes or so later, hand after hand tried Terry's door, and found it locked.

"Terry must have gone," said voice after voice. Joanna didn't enlighten them.

3

Terry the next day seemed none the worse for his second encounter with Neil Carter, although Joanna was able to observe him only at breakfast and lunch—he didn't play tennis and in the afternoon he went for a long solitary walk.

Unlike the Saturday before, she was so eager to see Neil Carter, detective, she was almost in Wincaster before she remembered Neil Carter the man with the sharp teeth, who had told her he fancied her. *That* Neil Carter, as well as the detective, had seen her holding hands with Terry Dawson, and as they would be eating, drinking and dancing together (she shivered), his witnessing of that insignificant event (oh, not insignificant, but not what Neil the travelling salesman would undoubtedly make of it) would be obtrusive between them. She thought she wanted him to be so obsessed with the unsolved murder that he would spend the entire evening as a detective. But even if he did he could be the kind of man in whom jealousy engendered meanness—a meanness which might run to deciding not to take her into his confidence about Vincent and Pam and the conversations he had had with Terry. Unless, of course, as a detective he had already decided that . . .

There was fortunately no time for further speculation. She had arrived and Neil was waiting at the door of *The Feathers,* as he had been waiting the last time, there was a space in the centre of the road and he opened the car door for her while she was still fiddling with the key. He was without smile or scowl and apparently relaxed, although he looked keenly into her face as she straightened up from the car. He put his hand, just firm, round her elbow in his usual way as he led her into the hotel, into the bar.

They sat down at the table where they had sat the week before, and there were so many possibilities—revelatory, embarrassing, alarming, exciting—Joanna's mind went expectantly and not unpleasantly blank and she concentrated on impressions, seeing Neil's pale face and the regular slight tic in his cheek, the decorations of the bar, the light shining on glass, with an unusual clarity.

"Drink as last week?"

She nodded. He gave her a second keen glance, but she wanted him to be the one to begin. The mood would be set by him, anyway, she would be foolish to make a start which could be false.

Neil was silent too until the drinks arrived and then he said, raising his glass to her,

"You look better and better."

"Yes, that's how I feel." Joanna returned the salute. She decided she was behaving childishly.

"How's it going?" she asked. "Are you getting anywhere, Neil?" She smiled, then so did he. The mood, at this stage of the evening at least, had after all been up to her, and she had almost thrown away the initiative. She made too many assumptions.

"I know some things I didn't know last Saturday." He grimaced. "I don't know how relevant they are, although perhaps the victim is beginning to come into focus."

"Are you going to tell me about them?"

"Yes. But not all of them quite yet. A hunch is forming."

She couldn't wait any longer.

"You'd already spoken to Terry Dawson when you came to his dressing-room last night?"

"I had. Yes." He gave nothing away.

"He had come to you."

"How did you know that?"

"Because I'd watched him"—she thought Neil's eyes briefly flickered—"and I saw he was worried—in the sort of way Vincent Bailey had been worried."

He nodded approvingly. His face was thinner and paler than it had been the week before.

"Are you going to tell me about that?"

"That's the thing I'm not going to tell you about yet."

"Oh, Neil!" Her disappointment was absurdly sharp.

"Only because—I think if I did tell you it would be unfair."

"Unfair?" She was agonisingly intrigued and it was infuriating to have the head waiter arrive and to have to choose her dinner. The second martinis came as the head waiter left.

"Yes, unfair," said Neil, as if there had been no interruption. "You see, I have this hunch. And if I'm right, what I can tell you about—Terry Dawson—belongs in a wider context."

"You mean—it would be unfair to Terry if you told me now?"

"I mean that, yes." He was watching her very closely, but without apparent malice. By "unfair to Terry" he must mean "unnecessarily unfair to your feelings about him, Joanna." And he needn't mean that, and he shouldn't mean it, he could only mean it in the wrong way.

Joanna took a long drink. There was something she had to say.

"You'll have realised that I like Terry Dawson. There is a rapport between us, we are mutually *sympathetique*." She was able to give an exaggerated stress to her words which she hoped made the truth of them soufflé-light. "That's why I asked you about him, because I mind about him more than the others. Although I mind about them all except Mrs. Berkeley."

She smiled at him steadily, and to her surprise he looked back at her in a concerned and kindly way. But she should know by now that his teeth showed when she least expected it, not when she was ready for them.

"Of course." Neil drained his glass and stood up, without suggesting the third martini which the previous Saturday she had refused.

The set-up in the dining-room was the same and the head waiter led them to the same table.

She waited through the first course, through the opening and serving of the wine. Then she said:

"Please start telling me what you're prepared to tell me."

He grinned. "When I've danced with you."

She preceded him between the tables, between candles fluttering with brief frenzy before the draught of their passage. As she turned round on the edge of the dance floor she found that of all the incipient sensations excitement predominated. Neil was watching her keenly again as his arms went round her—he was *detecting* her—and she stared back at him during her involuntary shivering response. It took her a few minutes to get a grip on herself and draw back a bit. Even with Peter she didn't dance cheek to cheek before the main course.

"Are you all right?" If it had been anyone but Neil Carter, she would have said he spoke tenderly.

"Yes."

With an effort she turned away from the abyss in her head which had opened ever so slightly again. The danger passed. The feeling of languor that remained, the pleasurable weakness in her limbs, that had been there before, it had overtaken her at the prospect of dancing with Neil. He knew it, of course. That, perhaps, was why he wasn't bothering with his travelling salesman act. Oddly enough she didn't mind him knowing it. It was amusing in a way, like a joke against herself. She grinned at him.

4

"Bailey came in on Tuesday morning," said Neil, almost before they had sat down, "sweating profusely."

"Poor Vincent." She was agog for what he would tell her. It was extraordinary to have two such totally different absorptions centred on one person and one evening.

"I didn't help him."

"Well, you wouldn't." He darted a look at her and she went on, only just serious-faced. "You'd have taken away his sense of moral superiority if you'd let him see that the game was up anyway."

"You should be in the force. Quite. I shan't attempt to reproduce the tossings about in the chair and the circumlocutions and the repetitions and the euphemisms . . ."

"Neil, please!"

He grinned. She thought he was enjoying himself. And possibly for the first time since the previous Saturday.

"Well. Apparently Julia had been something of a confidante to our Mr. Vincent. And during the course of his confidences he confided to her that he wanted to try and be—normal. But how to go about it? How to get the admixture of affection which would alone make it a fair trial? Julia I gather listened with much sympathy and eventually indicated—it seems in a very open, healthy, Doris Day sort of way—that she would be willing to initiate the lad in the ways of heterosexuality."

They neither of them had a sweet. They each leaned forward into the emptiness of the cleared table, small coffee cups between their elbows.

"Apparently they began a liaison."

"When? *Where?*" She thought indignantly of the Window.

"In her dressing-room, child. Always in her dressing-room. Love in the afternoon."

"And Vincent . . ."

"Like the man in Noël Coward's version of the Cole Porter song, he could *just* do it."

"Ernest Hemingway."

"Sorry?"

"Ernest Hemingway, he was the man in the song who could just do it."

They both laughed, because it really was rather funny, and Neil didn't laugh like the travelling salesman.

"Well, then," he said, "you see how it apparently was."

"And—what then?"

"Nothing then. They continued through the summer. It was still going on when she was killed. Intermittently."

"Did he learn—anything about her?"

"He doesn't think so. Well, nothing to shake his preconceived convictions of her goodness and kindness and generosity etcetera etcetera. I gather she was always the mentor and nurse. There was no development. Damn it, Joanna, there's nothing to help me, nothing!"

"Why did he tell Terry Dawson?"

"I think he got caught out one day and either had to prevaricate or tell Dawson, and he chose to tell him. I gather Dawson is rather easy to tell things to."

He was still staring at her. Joanna said lightly:

"That would be true. And now you have a hunch."

"Yes."

"Which is why you're not going to tell me yet about your conversations with Terry Dawson."

"Which is why. Oh, it's a wild enough idea." Neil flung himself back in his chair. A man and a woman were passing behind him, and a button on the man's jacket caught in his thick hair. That was funny, too, but Neil was impatient, unamused, while it was being disentangled. He said crossly, watching Joanna's mouth:

"For heaven's sake, laugh if you want to."

"I suddenly don't. There's nothing to bear out anything Vincent said, is there?"

"Nothing. Come and dance."

The evening appeared to be ending as it had ended the week before. Fewer candles, fewer people, less and slower movement. But when the music finally stopped he didn't kiss her, he moved back from her just far enough for there to be no contact and stared down at her, frowning. After a few seconds she turned and led the way back to the table. This time she had no intention of sitting down again. He picked up her bag and handed it to her.

"Time to go," she said.

"Joanna . . ." He held out his hand.

"I haven't told you anything about the week at *Seaview*, have I?" She heard her voice, businesslike. It was ridiculous to feel disappointed. And what about? "Not that I've really noticed anything new. Only that Vincent and Terry both seem the better for having talked to you, amazing as that is."

"Joanna . . ."

Something in his voice made her look at him properly, and he wasn't the detective, or the travelling salesman, or even the friend.

"Thank you for your hospitality," she said. Formality felt like a refuge. "This week I didn't earn it."

"Come upstairs and have a brandy," he said, "before you go."

They stared at one another. There were no clues in his face.

"Come on," he said.

"Aren't you tired?" she asked feebly, letting him take her by the elbow and lead her into the hall and up the wide shallow stairs.

"They do me quite nicely here," said Neil, unlocking a panelled door on the main landing. Inside was a sitting-room, with good furniture. "I don't feel in the last few days," he said as he switched on lamps, "that I've earned any hospitality either. Though actually this luxury is by courtesy of my chief, who set up the first lot of Yard inquisitions."

"He must think well of you."

"So far, perhaps."

"I know how you must feel. I wish I was helping you more."

She sat down in a comfortable chair. She was aware again of the paradox of her new selfishness, it made her think so little of herself, and with a new sharpness of what was outside her.

Neil came over from the towering mahogany cupboard with two small balloons of brandy. He gave her one and sat down in the chair opposite.

They didn't speak. Joanna expected to be tense, but she was relaxed, sipping her brandy, returning Neil's brooding gaze. When he got up and came over and stood in front of her she got up too, and smiled. He took her hand and led her into the other room and made love to her. She could not remember that it had ever been like that, gay and guiltless and affectionate. There was no sign of the travelling salesman. Her dismay that it should be so easy was a long way off.

"I think you took a great decision," said Neil. His face was too close for her to see it, but she sensed his grin.

"I didn't take a decision at all." Joanna heard her voice low and contented. "I used to take them, but not since I came to *Seaview*."

"That was the last decision, after which no others were necessary."

"Yes!"

When he said perceptive things like that, she got the same sort of regretful feeling about him which she had, somewhere always, for Peter.

He kissed her lightly.

"I hadn't thought," he said.

"What?"

"That you'd be—like you are."

"I don't know what I'm like, Neil, I really don't."

She was just aware of the abyss, the frailty of her well-being. He said, musingly:

"No, I don't think you do. I feel it's not only I who am learning about you. You're learning about yourself."

Vigilance again.

"You see too well for my comfort."

"Next Saturday?"

"Yes. Should you know then about your hunch?"

His arm tensed round her shoulders.

"Yes, I should know then. You'll see me around this week. I won't be popular."

"You aren't popular now."

He moved his head away, so that she could see his smile. His arm had relaxed again. He said:

"I would have expected you to make judgements on this."

"The murder?"

"No! Tonight. Now."

"So would I. Before coming to Linton I would have done. Only I wouldn't have been in your room in the first place, of course."

They both laughed. Neil said:

"It hasn't harmed you."

"On the contrary." But it had been an odd thing for him to say, to an older married woman. "What does Sergeant Diggory do when he isn't with you?" she asked lazily.

"Looks and listens. Checks and checks again. Liaises with the men who are watching everyone's comings and goings."

"Neil! I hadn't noticed . . ."

"I don't suppose you had."

"Yes, that was silly. By the way. I can't think how Pam's managing to keep so calm."

"Why shouldn't Pam be calm? She's the calm type *par excellence.*"

"Oh, I know. But with you questioning her about nearly confiding in me, even she . . . *Neil!*"

He was bolt upright and his hands were bruising her shoulders.

"Me—what? *I* don't know anything about Pam nearly confiding in you!" He was shaking her. "For heaven's sake, Joanna!"

"But I told you!"

"But you didn't, you told me nothing about Pam. Jesus wept, you've never mentioned the girl's name!"

She sat up too.

"But it was ages ago, on the tennis court . . ." She stopped for a moment, with the shock. "Oh, Neil, I remember now, last Saturday I *didn't* tell you. I came all ready to tell you and I told you some things, and I knew there was something else. You remember, I kept saying that . . ."

"You are the most—"

"And then somehow—I just assumed that I *must* have told you, it was so unusual, and the only thing that directly involved me—well, almost. I'm so sorry, I can still hardly believe . . ."

"Well, you better had. For God's sake get on with it."

She told him about Pam, on the tennis court, in the hotel afterwards, at Clare's party.

Neil listened stony-faced. Joanna found herself thinking *lèse-majesté,* that she really ought to cover up the bare chest under his grim official face. But she dare not smile and she wasn't really amused, she was too angry with herself.

"The only thing that looks like a real lead," said Neil, swinging his legs on to the floor and sitting hunched over his knees, "and you take a week to tell me."

"I find it harder than you do to realise myself such an idiot." She got off the bed and quickly dressed. Neil sat brooding all the time she was moving about the room, but when she was ready and went towards the door he got to his feet.

"There's something else you could say I learned this week," she said, "Brenda thinks Julia was a phoney."

He made no comment but pushed past her into the sitting-room and poured himself another tot of brandy. He didn't offer her any. He flung himself into a chair.

"You're not surprised. Did she tell you?"

"No. She merely implied that she thinks everyone is a phoney."

She went up to him and pulled his head back by the hair. He glared at her.

"You'll make it good," she whispered.

"You're right, I will."

"I'm ready to go."

Neil drained his glass and got slowly to his feet. He stumped back into the bedroom and came out fastening his shirt. She saw his sulky, schoolboy face in the mirror as he combed his hair.

The grandfather clock in the hall said a quarter past one. The night was still and starry, the air sharp enough to remind that summer was almost at an end. Neil took the keys out of her hand and unlocked the car. She got in quickly and he closed the door.

"Good luck!" she said, winding the window down. "I'm sorry."

"So you should be."

She saw him again through the mirror as she drove away, walking slowly back into the hotel, his hands in his pockets and his head bent.

On the way home, on the lonesome road, she lost her sense of innocence. She heard her voice, aloud and choked. It said:

"But Peter, you weren't here."

CHAPTER 15

I

Joanna heard the rain as she woke up, perhaps it wakened her. Heavy rain, lashed by wind against the hotel. There might have been winter curtains put up in her room since the day before. The word adultery came unwelcome as she lay listening to the rain, but her thoughts of her husband were more uncomfortable than painful. This was the only thing that really troubled her, that she was not troubled more, but even this was not devastating because the sense of innocence had returned, the feeling that she had obeyed a natural law at a due time. Despite herself she lay relaxed and contented until she heard the crackling of her paper, jibbing as it did on Sundays from its girth at Margaret's attempts to push it under her door.

The headline was rain, which had started in London in time to be news. Last Sunday's prayers for rain (Thelma had told them about these prayers, charmingly, on her return from church) had finally been answered, and in areas of the north they had been answered violently, and a man and a sheep had been struck by lightning.

Joanna drew the curtains back. Rain at Linton although fierce, sweeping across the empty promenade, shrouding the horizon in mist and forcing the high edge of the tide into the air in pale grey droplets against the dark grey sky, had defeated summer quietly and without artillery. But what an enormous, a total, defeat, even if, as one hoped in September, it was a battle which had been lost rather than the war. The excited female voices rising through the Window expressed the drama of the change, and Joanna skimped her dressing to get downstairs and see what was going on.

Clare, Pam and the Berkeley girls were just inside the open front door, exclaiming with Rhoda, Gail and Brenda, who were just outside and holding their faces up to the soaking wind. Joanna watched them all unobserved, struck by the division into those who watched the rain from the comfort of the porch and those who exposed themselves to it. It was a case-book illustration of their dispositions. Rhoda, Gail and Brenda were the three, of course, who wouldn't worry about getting their feet wet literally or metaphorically, or disturbing their hair (and this was why Gail was so especially nice, because she liked to have her hair just so). Her tendrils were already dark, pressed against her temples and hanging below her earrings. Brenda gave a small sensuous shake of her narrow shoulders under the rain. Rhoda's arms and long feet and mouth were spread wide. When Thelma came downstairs she of course remained with the group in the hall and Joanna would not have been surprised to learn that she had practised her little exclamations of surprise and dismay before leaving her room.

The dining-room at breakfast seemed smaller than usual, more enclosed, perhaps because the eyes were halted now at the bursts of dull spray above the sea wall and the inner world had contracted with the outer. All speech seemed a little too loud and once when Mrs. Berkeley's voice rose high and harsh Terry leaned across and put his hand a moment on her arm, until she subsided: he had recovered his concern for his players. Joanna realised that she had not been looking forward to seeing Terry, in her knowledge of the night before, but she found she was not disturbed in the way she had feared (what was that?), only that her hovering sense of regret—for Peter? for Neil? for herself?—deepened when she looked at him and something indefinable tugged at her heart.

She went and stood in the front doorway after breakfast, breathing the moist air, and bumped against Delia as she turned back into the hall.

"You look happy, Joanna," said Delia, peering at her curiously. In another ten years, Delia in profile would be looking like Punch.

"I suppose I am."

She supposed she was, but that was not really why she had been smiling when she collided with Delia. She had been smiling because she had noticed the drops of water on her hands and arms, which she had held out to the open air, and had remembered her reflections on the girls. *She* had not got wet, but nor had she kept entirely dry. Following Delia into the lounge she wondered if that had been the trouble, if that had been what had sent her, in the bitter end, to *Seaview*.

Joanna shook herself irritably, as she sat trying to read her paper, to shake herself out of such facile philosophising. The weather was to blame, turning her into her own head. It was an opportunity to turn her to her fellow-guests, they were nearly all there, deep in easy chairs and sofas with their papers, as much off their guard as she would ever see them.

But Vincent wasn't looking at his paper, he was staring fascinated at the door. Joanna followed his gaze. Detective Inspector Carter was standing there, weekday-suited, quietly, politely, waiting, but giving out an impression of something less than deference. He stood there without moving, as one face after another rose from its reading. The silence changed, charged. Susie or Sonia or Sandra slipped off the arm of the chair where she was reading over her sister's shoulder, and choked back her exclamation of shock.

Joanna looked round very quickly, but of course not quickly enough to catch instinctive reactions, even Vincent's had given way to that firming of the features she had seen him practising when he was gathering courage to approach Neil. Pam was half smiling, but there was a trace of colour in her face. Rhoda, along with Brian and Mrs. Berkeley, looked hostile. Everybody waited.

Neil's voice was more conciliatory than his presence. He said mildly:

"That's convenient, you're nearly all here. Mrs. Tompkins has put the back office at our disposal again. I have Divisional Detective Inspector Hargreaves with me. You know him, I think." He looked thoughtfully round them. Most of the newspapers were now on the floor or crushed down the sides of chairs and sofas. Without having noticeably pulled themselves up from their relaxed Sunday positions they were all tense, Joanna saw it in their hands and eyes.

"We'll start with Mr. Bluemkrot," said Neil, nodding at Dirk, and Delia gave out a choked and dramatic *"Liebchen!"* Dirk patted her hand a couple of times and smiled uncertainly at them all before following Neil Carter out into the hall. Delia looked fiercely and defiantly round the lounge. "He is only *starting* with my brother!" she said aggressively. Sergeant Diggory stood in the hall, looking impassively in on them.

2

It was black Sunday. Neil Carter and Inspector Hargreaves interviewed everyone, even including Gail, relentlessly through the day, breaking only for a half-hour lunch and a ten-minute tray of tea. They kept Pam for longer than they kept anyone else, but Joanna thought she was the only one to notice this, and they kept everyone for a considerable time. On emerging one of the Berkeley girls wept, Brian swaggered, Arthur looked as frail as paper. Everyone looked as if he or she had been through the mill. The rain maintained its diagonal lash without a break throughout the day.

Lunch was a glum affair. Only Delia and two of the Berkeley girls tried to get conversation going, but they started on an uncomfortably high note and soon lapsed from lack of support. Neil and Inspector Hargreaves lunched together in silence. The divisional inspector looked amiable and was on the stout side. Joanna guessed that the questioning was taking a form devised by the younger man. Before he left the dining-room Neil came over to her and said politely, looking coldly into her eyes:

"I regret all this on your account, Mrs. Stuart, but I am glad to see that you are not letting it chase you away from the lounge." For a second his eyes supported his message.

"That's quite all right, Inspector, of course you have to do your duty." She gave him back his look. "I've no intention of being driven away, I assure you."

She turned from him to see Terry watching her and felt the stretch of her hasty overwide smile. He nodded, with what reached her as chill, and this was so unwelcome and unaccustomed she waited to leave the dining-room until he rose, and walked out beside him.

"I'm sorry about everything," she said, putting her hand on his arm.

"We're all sorry," said Terry, moving slightly but deliberately so that he escaped her touch. He nodded again, formally, and went upstairs.

Joanna's instinct was to go upstairs too, and sit in the Window or lie on the bed and try to wrap herself up against the draught which

Terry's coldness had set blowing round her. But she was dizzy and might not make it, and she went and sat in the lounge.

Her inevitable first thought, because of the coincidence of this change in Terry with her visit to Wincaster, was to blame Neil Carter, but she dismissed it almost as it came, as much because she simply could not believe he would kiss and tell, as for the practical reason that he had not yet summoned Terry, hadn't spoken to him since Friday night.

Yet Terry had snubbed her, so it must be that he had started to regret what had grown up between them.

And what for heaven's sake was that? Joanna moved to a seat where she could see the whole room, watch them going to their interrogations, and coming back. It was absurd, to be feeling such a sense of loss.

3

The detectives finished at seven o'clock. Dinner had been put back. The two inspectors came into the lounge before leaving.

"Thank you all for your patience and co-operation," said Detective Inspector Hargreaves politely.

"We shall want to see some of you again, but we'll let you know," said Neil.

"Is this leading anywhere?" asked Rhoda aggressively, almost horizontal in her chair, moving no more than her mouth.

"The solution is here," said Neil, no less politely than Hargreaves, looking slowly round the room, "so that each time we are in contact with you, we are closer to it."

There was an uncomfortable silence. Joanna saw Terry bite his lip. He had been in and out of the lounge during the afternoon, but he had not looked towards her and his rebuff had made her wary. In the slight relaxation of tension which followed the sight of the inspectors going down the path, getting into their car and driving away (the silence was prolonged while everybody watched the process), when the bell was being rung for Margaret and drinks ordered, her presiding emotion, which was still disbelief, sent her across the room to where Terry was sitting. It was horrible to feel selfconscious about Terry, but the casual way in which she asked him if he was going to the *Imperial* was a product of her will.

Terry said, with a brief cold glance, "You must excuse me this evening."

Joanna went upstairs then, no longer in any doubt, and into her room and across to the Window.

She had no more thought that it might be Neil Carter. It was she herself, when she had flung her arms round Terry's neck. She had thought his surprise was the surprise of pleasure, but he had had time to think about it. And she must think about it too, and accept that their relationship (what relationship?) had been too frail to absorb the gesture.

Joanna stood at the Window for a long time, fiercely reminding herself that it had been her grail, of how she had sought and found it and changed during the voyage, putting on courage and joy like shining armour. Nothing and nobody could take these away from her, they could be lost only if she herself abandoned them.

And there was the new grateful, daily acknowledgement of being alive and well . . .

By the time the gong sounded she thought she felt better, and had changed her dress and begun again on her face. She went along with a diminished party to the *Imperial*—no Terry, no Dirk or Delia, no Berkeleys, no Brian. No Pam. Arthur and Robbie did the honours, Robbie's honest face creased with anxiety and regret about the whole business. Arthur and Rhoda bounced sallies off each other for a few moments in their old way, almost in the routine they employed in one of the shows, but this soon lapsed. Arthur gave them another little pep talk which didn't make any noticeable difference to them but which Joanna felt helped a bit, if only because it was so much easier to admit the fact that they were worried and unhappy, so much less of a strain. As the evening drifted on, marked by more drinks and less modification of behaviour than the week before, unless they became more obviously gloomy, she looked for a few escaping fragments of what had gone on between each of them and the inspectors.

She found nothing. The only effect of their visit was that Rhoda's depression was now almost visible, hanging in her heavy untidy hair, Brenda seemed to take up less space than ever, Gail looked all the time for small opportunities of self-abasement (like setting herself up for Brenda to knock down) as if in that way she could make up for her involuntary freedom from fear. Joanna found it worrying to look at Arthur—he was so incredibly frail, when his features fell into repose she wondered if they would ever reanimate, she could imagine his body folding away beneath him like the bodies of the human dolls he never used. But he had more spirit than the rest of them put together, and just kept them afloat. He was almost angry with his friend Rhoda when she muttered that it would have been better not to have come.

"What help would you have afforded, my dear young lady, to yourself or to any of the rest of us," demanded Arthur reproachfully, "if you had not come out this evening?"

"I think we would be better, now," said Rhoda defiantly, "to go into separate cubicles and stay there, except for stage purposes, until we all disperse for good in two weeks' time. It would hurt less."

"The goal of the least hurt," said Arthur, "is not always the goal to pursue. And anyway, Rhoda love"—his teeth flashed out, his moving hand fluttered briefly on to her arm—"the damage is done, the concern has already grown."

"Yes," said Rhoda miserably.

"Ye know," said Robbie, "we may not be all dispairsing in two weeks' time. Tha' depends."

"Gail will disperse," said Rhoda, and "That was unnecessary!" said Gail hotly, and Joanna and Arthur said, on an instant, *"Please!"* and Arthur went on to entreat them not to get at one another, or to feel their predicament filled the world.

When they came out of the *Imperial* the rain had stopped, and there was a warm wet south wind. Joanna walked home, with Robbie, Brenda and Gail, in silence along the gleaming promenade.

4

Life went on during the week ostensibly as it had gone on the week before, although the atmosphere was edgy and occasionally explosive. Neil Carter was seen no more at *Seaview*, but people sometimes said they had to go out immediately after breakfast, or immediately after lunch, or at some time when they had contracted to do something, and they broke their previous engagements without offering any explanation. Pam did this twice, and although she continued as creamy-skinned, as imperturbable, as ever, Joanna saw a tightening of her facial muscles, a slight contraction of the mouth, which spoke of onslaught and siege. Had Pam given way? Joanna could hardly wait for Saturday evening, and now on all counts. She had stood at the Window and wrapped herself up as well as she could against the cold of Terry's withdrawal, but Neil would offer an extra blanket and forbid her for a while, by the insistence of his presence, to notice the draught. By the end of the week Joanna was avoiding Terry, except for mornings on the tennis courts where there was no opportunity for regret except in the arriving and departing. When rain stopped play she sat alone under the glass dome of the Winter Gardens drinking coffee and listening to the alternate brass and strings. She was about to ask Gail for a ticket for the third show but on Thursday after breakfast Terry handed her one, scarcely interrupting his journey across the hall.

There was as much pain as pleasure in watching the performance—and additionally because Arthur seemed below par and once or twice briefly lost the thread of his routine—and when she went backstage afterwards she went to the girls' dressing-room and stayed there. She noticed Gail looking at her particularly, as if to make sure she was really still there and hadn't gone across the corridor. When they got back to *Seaview* she could feel Gail's question coming and she excused herself and ran upstairs and got into bed, where her dullness of spirit acted like a drug and sent her to sleep.

The rain held off for the later part of the week, although the fine weather did not return with its earlier pastel certainty. The sky now was a closer, deeper blue, the sun more golden, but it disappeared from time to time behind clouds, and Joanna drove to Wincaster on Saturday evening through a landscape which changed in the twinkling of an eye from flatness and greyness to brilliant colour with sharp black shadows, and back again.

Neil met her as usual by the car, and Joanna no longer began the evening by trying to deny to herself that the first touch of his hand brought a weakness in her limbs. Over drinks Neil talked about himself, about his early youth and about joining the Force, and forbore to ask her questions in exchange.

They were half-way through dinner before she asked him the key question.

"Did your hunch pay off?"

"Yes. *Yes*."

Neil flung himself back in his chair and grinned at her as his head, this time without subsequent entanglement, came into sharp contact with a passing body.

"Tell me?"

"It isn't easy," he said, uncharacteristically hesitant.

"I'm patient and understanding."

"I'm sure you are. It's not that." He seemed to be eating more, but each plate that was taken away from in front of him was still strewn with food. "All right, here goes, then. My hunch was to ask each man, gently, to tell me about his affair with Julia. Not 'Did you?', you understand, but taking it as read, just wanting the why and wherefore filling in."

She could only stare at him.

"When Terry Dawson came to me last week, it was to tell me that he had slept with Julia."

There were so many emotions they jammed together into a numbness, and she took in what Neil had said merely with her mind. But she still couldn't speak.

"He told me he'd lately lost his wife." He could have been looking at her very carefully. "Well, Julia was sorry for him—and it happened. Dawson seemed—surprised by what he was telling me, as if he couldn't really believe it, as if it was as unlikely after it happened as before. He had taken it as a sort of a friendly gesture and implied that he'd been relieved as well as acceptant when the gesture wasn't repeated. At any rate the old pre-experience relationship was resumed, he told me. He said he'd always known he ought to tell me about it and not rely on his own judgement that it had no bearing on the murder, and after he'd persuaded Bailey to talk to me about *his* experience, his conscience got the upper hand, and he came."

They paused while the table was cleared and coffee brought. Joanna lit another cigarette.

"Does Vincent know about—Terry and Julia?" she asked Neil.

"You shouldn't smoke so much. Dawson says not and I've no reason to disbelieve that. And Julia didn't talk. I know that because I found out that every man jack of them with the exception of the old ventriloquist had shared Dawson's experience. And each one thought he was the one and only, thought she treated every man as a person rather than a man, with the exception of that one radiant, wonderful time she singled him out."

"One . . . time?"

"Well, two at the most. Absolutely no more. She just went back, in each case, to being her breezy, friendly self and there wasn't a blamed thing he could do about it. Anyway, she'd made each of them think she was conferring a unique privilege, I gather from between the lines, and they thought they'd already had more than they deserved. No, the only chap who got beyond that tight little pattern was our friend Vincent Bailey. He really was struggling along in some kind of semi-regular liaison."

"And no one knew about that either, except for Terry Dawson?"

"No one, it seems. And Dawson tells me he didn't know of it when he . . . well, he couldn't have done, because he seems to have been the first—victim, I was going to say, but Madame Julia was the victim."

"Vincent—came later?"

"He came later than Dawson. I gather he ran alongside, as it were, most of the others."

"You said Arthur . . ."

"Arthur was outraged."

"He's in show business . . ."

"Oh, I know all that. But this was genuine. The most genuine outrage *I've* ever seen. He threatened to report me to my 'superior' for abusing my privileged position with my obscene suggestion. I had to calm him down. He was—well, he was disgusted."

"Not Robbie Ross."

"I've told you, all of them. She was sorry for him when he had a few down days, and it happened. Likewise Dirk—yes! A classic case of sex-starvation, Dirk . . ."

"The orchestra? Jake and Charlie?"

"I had no reason to question them." She thought he sounded regretful.

"Not Brian. Surely not Brian."

"*Et tu* Brian. He was the only one, incidentally, who wasn't confused, just told me what I asked him, with complete composure. Said when I asked him why the hell he hadn't told me of his own accord, that it had no bearing on the murder. Conceited little prig!"

"Oh, Neil, I'm sorry for you!" She *was* smoking too much, her throat was dry and her voice husky. "But perhaps it cuts out the possibility of a murderess?"

"Perhaps it doesn't. If one of the women was fancying one of the men, and knew . . . God, the whole thing's wider open than it's ever been, one ripe juicy motive after another!"

"The thing that hits me is how extraordinarily clever Julia must have been!"

"Up to a point only, because eventually she got herself killed."

"Well, yes, but to juggle as she did and not drop anything and leave such an atmosphere behind. So—well, so chummy!"

"I know," he said gloomily.

"Neil—where did it all happen?"

"In her dressing-room, dear. After the show. When the rest of them had gone home. She had her own car, and from the start she established a reputation for liking cosy little chats *à deux*. Sometimes she asked one of the girls to stay behind with her. No," he said quickly, "I don't think anything of that kind happened with the girls. And other times she asked one of the men and, to repeat myself, each one thought himself uniquely privileged."

"And Julia hid her tally stick."

"Just so."

"And of course they all still categorically deny that they killed her."

"Categorically, every man jack of them. And every woman. Over again."

"And do you believe them all, Neil?"

"Dammit, none of them has let slip anything that makes me inclined not to believe them—and with none of them have I had an *instinct*. I tend to get an instinct somewhere in a case."

"You've had it," pointed out Joanna unhelpfully. "You had it when you taxed them all with having affairs with Julia. It was a brilliant instinct."

"I do have another idea. I *have* to have."

He looked at her pretty desperately and she held out her hand and he followed her on to the dance floor. She didn't ask him any more about the murder until just before she got ready to leave his rooms.

"What's your latest idea? And what about Pam?"

She felt the tightening of his arm behind her head.

"I hoped you were going to forget about Pam."

"Why?"

"Because she's part of the idea I've got and I'm going to be secretive again."

"So you broke her down?"

"I did," he said complacently, kissing her.

"So she could have told me something."

There was nothing strange, everything inevitable, about physical contact with Neil. Perhaps that was why she couldn't feel guilty. Sometimes she tried.

"I think she would only have asked your advice, about whether to come to me."

"So she had a conscience too."

"Let's say she has a practical side which didn't much like seeing a good lead going to waste."

"A good lead."

"God, I don't know." His arm behind her head was like steel. "I've got to do something, soon."

"And you won't tell me?"

"At the moment I'll only tell you that, in corny classic style, I'm going to stage a reconstruction of the murder, and that I want you to be there, *looking*."

"But if you told me where to look . . ."

"And if I'm way off beam you'd be looking in the wrong direction. No, I want you to beware of them all."

"When's it going to be?"

"Next Thursday, after second house. When it happened. I'll tell them tomorrow. One of them knows already. Gail. She'll be there unofficially too. I've asked her to tell you what to do. Of course you'll be amazed when she approaches you."

"Of course."

"Joanna, don't go yet . . ."

CHAPTER 16

I

Neil's Sunday visit, that week, lasted only the length of time it took him to brief them about the reconstruction of Julia's murder, and it didn't rain. But gloom and unease were even more observable, and the *Imperial* party even smaller than it had been the week before. This time Terry joined it and Joanna didn't.

During the week, the last of *Summer Time,* she walked a lot, on her own, or sat in the Window. In the first astonishingly happy days at *Seaview* she could not have believed that, when the time came, she would have so little regret at the prospect of being left alone. She would miss the tennis, the mystery—which would be either solved or shelved—the presence round her of so much life, but she would be content to read and walk and think about the next stage in her transformed existence. Melancholy would fog the edges of things for a while, but she wouldn't weaken, to Daphne or to anyone else. She would probably go to London and see Neil Carter.

The sea food shop by the pier had closed, the four donkeys had trotted away for the last time, the petunias had been lifted from the centre of the promenade. Joanna bathed a couple more times, in a boisterous sea which whipped and warmed her skin, then ran straight back into the hotel because the sun no longer dried her. There were fewer people on the beach now, and in the town, and the population was older. Joanna began to be aware of the native folk of Linton. One faded pretty woman with a stick and a silent white-moustachioed husband told her in the *Marigold* how much she was looking forward to the return of her friend for the winter to one of the small hotels like *Seaview.* Joanna learned that the influx of the narrow-circumstanced elderly took place during the first week in October, as precisely as the start of an academic year. Then, she supposed, *Seaview* would begin to look like that private hotel where she had visited her aunt so long ago, one wary-eyed old figure to one table.

Yet the prospect failed to dismay her. Several times, as she walked about the quietening town or sat in the Window, she tried to make herself afraid, to test the bounds of her courage, and she was unable to find them. Peter, her house with the plants and flowers which Joe might not be watering, Terry's defection, the imminence of solitude, all these things left her courage intact. It might be a negative sort of courage, made possible by what felt like a slight blunting of her nerve ends, but at least it enabled her to enjoy the small things which increasingly would make up the days.

"The end of *Summer Time* marks the end of summer," observed Brenda on Wednesday afternoon, across a table in the *Marigold*. Joanna had come upon her by chance, and joined her. "Do you feel it?"

"Very strongly."

"There's an elegiac note to the end of season at the seaside," said Brenda, "a very gentle dying fall. I find it attractive. You can look both ways: back to the vigour of the summer, and forward to the life of the winter, robust in quite a different way. Seaside in the winter isn't really melancholy, only the autumn transition."

"It's as if people are waiting for the last night of the show, and then it really will be over."

"They are, and it will."

Joanna caught sight of Gail—she was always, now, half looking out for Gail—peering at her through the long window. Gail came into the café. She checked slightly on seeing Brenda too, but advanced to the table.

"May I?"

Joanna said, "Of course!" and Brenda inclined her head.

Gail looked agitated.

"You're not worrying about tomorrow, are you?" asked Brenda, in faint amusement. "You won't even be there."

Gail gave her a reproachful look, her eyes unnaturally bright. Joanna knew now for certain how much Gail hated not belonging.

"Don't take it personally," said Brenda to Gail, "but I must be off."

"I don't somehow understand her," said Gail, as Brenda went past the window.

"Well, no, you wouldn't, nor she you, I don't suppose."

Show business was a strange business, yoking two people like Gail and Brenda in artistic harness.

Joanna watched Gail while their tea things were unloaded from the waitress's tray, but covertly because she was not supposed to be waiting for anything.

"I'm not in the show tomorrow, as you'll have gathered from Brenda," said Gail, when the waitress had gone.

"It's a real reconstruction, then."

"Yes," said Gail glumly. "And—Joanna, Inspector Carter wants you to do something."

"Me? What on earth do you mean?"

It was the first time she had seen Gail flushed.

"*I've* got to do something. Well, he asked me to, and he said it would help to get at the truth, and he asked me to ask you—for the same reason. He said he thought you'd be willing when you knew it would help . . . Oh, Joanna, it's hateful, hateful!"

"Tell me about it, please, Gail."

"Sorry." Gail blew her nose and drank some tea. "I feel so *disloyal,*" she said.

"That's natural. But tell me . . ."

"Sorry. He's asked me to get myself up as Julia and—play the corpse. Yes!" Gail looked at Joanna as if expecting to be challenged.

"Oh, Gail. That's not a bit nice." She didn't have to pretend to be surprised about that. "But of course it *will* help, especially if—you're going to try and look like Julia?"

"I can look exactly like her," said Gail despondently, "I'm awfully good at make-up and she had a wig for when her hair needed doing."

"Ne—Inspector Carter must be truly thankful. What can he want *me* to do?"

"He wants you to be sort of stationed in the doorway between Julia's dressing-room and the props room so that when Sonia screams and they rush in you'll see their faces when they see me. The Inspector says they won't be expecting a corpse, much less one that really looks like Julia. You must see without being seen, and nobody's to know that we've gone to the theatre."

"Easier said than done?"

"We're to be at the stage door at 9:15. That's just as they've all gone on stage for the Dutch routine. The police will come to the door and hurry us through to Julia's room and we'll lock ourselves in. They'll have been buzzing round all evening, ever since first house, so everyone will expect Julia's dressing-room to be sealed off. Nobody will know we're there." Gail looked anxiously at Joanna. "You'll come with me, won't you, Joanna? Inspector Carter will brief you properly when we get there. But you'll come?"

"I'll come," said Joanna slowly. Her reluctance was not assumed.

2

Terry came up to Joanna in the hall after lunch on Thursday, holding out the familiar piece of yellow paper.

"We hope you'll come," he said, "on Saturday this week. It's the last night."

The plural pronoun stung for a moment.

"Thanks," said Joanna. There were a few splashes of rain multiplying on the hall windows. She went upstairs and lay on the bed and thought of the room in winter, with a pile of interesting books at her side and a few delicate, understated friendships among the new clientele. Then she thought about if Neil had been there with her, and then inescapably of Neil directing them backstage later that evening . . .

It was impossible to relax, the nervousness was running through the building. The voices she could hear were nervous, and the sudden laughter. Feet, a number of them, seemed to be stamping about on the front step. Joanna jumped off the bed in relief at the distraction and when she could see nothing from the Window except that the rain had stopped she ran downstairs.

Miss Waterhouse was standing in the hall attempting to shepherd everybody outside. Photographic equipment hung from her neck by several straps, and she was flushed with the excitement of the hunter in sight of his quarry. Joanna felt a shock at the ineptitude of the timing, but Miss Waterhouse might know nothing of the evening's proposed activity.

Her bright eyes clouded as they fell on Joanna.

"Oh, Mrs. Stuart," said Miss Waterhouse flatly. "Every year I make a photographic record of our players . . . There is a place on the office wall . . . In the ten years I have been at *Seaview* I haven't missed . . ."

"Miss Waterhouse, I have no intention of trying to join the party!" Joanna smiled reassuringly at the photographer, pushed gently through the group in the doorway and went down the rest of the steps. She looked back at them from the lawn as they assembled. Miss Waterhouse had clearly made appointments, because everyone was there. Joanna moved her eyes systematically along the two rows of them as they waited almost motionless for Miss Waterhouse, rising and sinking with alarming suppleness on the path, to take half a dozen shots.

At the back the tallest: Robbie with an obliging natural smile, Brian blank, Terry grave, the three Berkeley girls flashing smiles at the last minute, each time, out of the white intensity of their faces, Vincent smiling selfconsciously and giving a calculated turn to his head, Rhoda looking so magnificently energetic that when the pictures were developed she would seem to have been caught in mid-movement. And in front of them Arthur grinning mirthlessly, Mrs. Berkeley also baring her teeth, Delia and Dirk holding hands and choosing to look coyly at each other, Thelma (in the precise centre of the picture) smiling delightfully, Clare pale and serious, Brenda looking sideways over the sea, Gail large-eyed, Pam as ever.

"The light is *perfect!*" squeaked Miss Waterhouse, not once but several times. "Try not to screw up your eyes!"

As she finished a cloud wiped out the sun, and there was the flat sepia picture against its sepia surround as it would eventually hang, thought Joanna, in the office at *Seaview*. She would go and look at it, wondering if she had once been dreaming.

It wasn't cold but she saw two of the Berkeley girls shiver as they all went silently indoors, and when Joanna followed them in and Gail reached back and took her hand, she saw goose-flesh on Gail's arm.

Miss Waterhouse's tumult had still not quite subsided an hour later, when she came to tell Joanna she was wanted on the telephone. Joanna thought it would be Neil Carter, and it was.

"You've seen Gail?"

"Yes."

"Bring her in the car and be at the stage door at 9:15 sharp. You know I don't want you to be seen?"

"Yes."

"All right, then?"

"I suppose so. Good luck."

As she put the receiver down Joanna realised that she hadn't for a moment wondered if the call might be from her husband.

3

Gail came to sit at Joanna's table for dinner. Neither of them ate or talked much. They couldn't talk about anything except what was to happen at the theatre, and this would have been lunatic with Mrs. Tompkins and Miss Waterhouse so obviously alert. They had the lounge to themselves for coffee, and afterwards Joanna suggested they should go and lie on their beds until it was time to leave. But Gail begged in vehement alarm not to be left alone and so the two of them stayed slumped in their corner of the lounge until almost nine o'clock, falling eventually into a nervous doze. They left themselves with only just enough time to get ready, and Gail told Margaret that if anybody rang she and Mrs. Stuart had gone out for a drink. Mrs. Tompkins tried to hold them back with some unaccustomedly gracious talk over the office counter about Joanna's plans, and there were a tense few moments as Joanna tried to extricate herself. In the end Gail rescued her with the apparent onset of a tantrum from the doorway. This Mrs. Tompkins understood, and she hastily sent them on their way.

The act seemed to have put slight new heart into Gail.

"I'm trying to remember that I'll be in London on Sunday," she said as they drove along the promenade, "even if they hate me for what I'm doing."

"Even if they hate you, which they won't, you must remember that."

"Whatever I remember, I still feel so beastly treacherous."

"You couldn't have refused, and you'd be feeling ghastly now if you had, far, far, worse."

She drove past the stage door and saw the dark figure. When she parked a few yards away it showed up by her window.

"You're late."

"We're not, but we would have been if it hadn't been for Gail."

"No, you weren't late," said Neil, when the three of them were safely locked into Julia's dressing-room, each drinking a small measure of whisky which Neil had poured out, feeling ludicrously cosy for the first few moments of relief, in the deep upholstery and under the soft pools of lamplight. "You were spot on. It just seemed a long time, waiting outside and thinking about those lengths of corridor back to here."

"Have you rehearsed with them," asked Gail, "what they did—the first time?"

"Oh, yes. Between them—all but one!—they've dug out their memories and now they think they remember. Nobody admits to coming to Julia's dressing-room until about twenty minutes after *The Queen*, so we've got quite a long war of nerves."

"And you say," asked Joanna, "that no one—officially—went into the props room either?"

"That's right. And you needn't go into it until the last minute."

"That's something."

"When you do go, I want you to stand close against the connecting door . . . you know the set-up in there?"

"Yes." There was an unwelcome pang as she remembered Terry showing her.

"If you look through the door into here you look straight towards the outside door of this room. Which means that when they all crowd in following Sonia Berkeley's scream of discovery you'll see each man and woman jack of them and I want you to *watch*. Keep incognito in the dark doorway, and go out through the main props room door on to the corridor and home. No waiting for Gail of course, who by then will not be incognito. You needn't pass Julia's dressing-room to get out, you can turn left and then take that little door at the end and the passage twists back to the stage door. Fred'll have gone."

It wasn't so difficult, acting as if she had hardly met Neil Carter, because from the start they had had two relationships, and in both of them they had been astringent. Gail anyway, when she had finished her whisky and smoked a couple of cigarettes (every so often Neil flapped his arms ostentatiously against the women's cigarette smoke), began to move away from them into the artistic experience which was the turning of herself into the dead Julia. She went behind the screen first, and put on the silver uniform of the finale. Then she placed a blown-up photo of Julia on the dressing-table beside her, pushed away her tendrils, and bound her elaborate coiffure with a white band. She worked steadily, and steadily and perceptibly her face changed. It grew smaller and rosier, the eyes rounder, the cheek-bones less prominent, the mouth smaller and fuller. When the short brown Julia-curls were lowered on to her brow they finally banished Gail, and Julia smiled winningly and bracingly at her photograph.

Neither Neil nor Joanna had ever met Julia, but their reactions were both extreme. Neil grinned as he recovered.

"Oh, boy!" he said. "Oh, boy, oh, boy, oh, boy."

Julia was no longer smiling and the unhappy stare into the mirror was Gail, peering macabrely through the winsome Julia features. Julia could never have looked so uncertain.

"Now to kill her," said Gail.

She injured her neck first, with reds and purples. When she had done, it looked bruised and swollen as well as highly coloured. Then she coated Julia's health with a pale powder, strategically empurpled. "At the last moment," she said, and so clever had she been that Joanna was amazed her voice came out undamaged, "I'll put some purple on my tongue, and stick it out." All at once she was Gail at her most confident, concentrating on the job in hand, and now the outer and the inner had reversed their roles, so that Gail's excitement filtered gruesomely through Julia's death mask . . .

It was ten o'clock, and they had wound down to immobility and silence. Gail still sat before the dressing-table, but held her monstrous head to one side. Joanna was curled in a corner of the sofa, smoking, Neil on the upright chair. They stayed like that until a quarter past ten, until they heard the cast finally pour back off the stage. Neil got up then, so quietly Joanna jumped, unlocked the door through to the props room and beckoned her.

"Sergeant Diggory will unlock the props room door from outside in a few moments," he said, when she was standing beside him, "when it's too late for anyone to go in there, should anyone be so perverse as to try. He's cleared a passage for you."

He briefly flooded the props room with light and she saw the route to the main door. The inner door opened outwards into Julia's dressing-room. Open only a few inches it gave her a full framed view of the door on to the corridor. Having placed her, Neil went and stood with his back to that door, looking frowningly towards her. He came back.

"If you don't move," he said, "you won't be spotted. Just stand and watch, until you've registered every gut reaction, then slip away through the props room and scarper home. And maybe get a pen and paper out as soon as you get back before things fade—that is, if something hasn't shrieked at you."

"Where will you be?"

"Behind the screen at first."

They were whispering, because of the mood rather than from any necessity, behind those stout doors.

"All right?" Neil hesitated, then said quickly, "When you get back, lock your bedroom door and stay there until the morning. Until everyone's up and about."

"Neil!"

"Not to worry, really. Just to be sensible." He softly kissed her cheek. Gail hissed, from round the corner, making Joanna jump again,

"I'm going to lie down. Please come and arrange me!"

Neil nodded to Joanna and disappeared. Now she could see nothing of what was happening in the dressing-room, she could see only a stretch of brown carpet leading to the door, and the door itself. Her heart was very loud. In a few moments she heard the sharp click of the key unlocking the door behind her, the door outlined by the corridor light and on the far side of baskets and coat racks and ottomans which Sergeant Diggory might have pushed aside but which in the dark through which she must stumble were still hazards. She was aware of that unlocked door behind her now, even though Neil had assured her it was so hung that if it was opened the line of light would pass her by. From the dressing-room she heard the murmur of Neil's and Gail's voices, then from before and behind there was silence.

A few more minutes or seconds, and Joanna had to look away from the bright door across the carpet because it had dissolved in a blur. But when the knock came, and Sonia's face inquiring into the room, she was able to take in every detail in sharp focus. Sonia consciously lowered her eyes to the carpet, to the spot where she had unconsciously lowered them before, but the horror in her face and the peal after peal of dreadful screaming could have been no more intense the first time. The urgency of it brought a precipitation of feet which Joanna thought was not entirely voluntary, the faces that now crowded the doorway were not entirely acting. Motionless, she watched them avidly. The narrowness of the doorway meant that the revelation of Gail broke on them only in twos and threes, giving her the chance to see every face before it could recover.

Violent reaction in each, of course, horror, fear, shrinking. Nothing more.

But, yes, oh God, hatred, naked hatred, fierce and yet afraid, like the picture of Satan at bay she had once seen in a nineteenth-century engraving.

So blinding was this hatred Joanna raised her arm to ward it off, and the eyes from which it blazed were caught by the movement and looked up into her own. It was only for one or two seconds, it might not have happened at all, the eyes might have been dazzled by the brilliance of the dressing-room lights and unable to penetrate the shadows. Almost at once they had veered aside, to fasten on Neil Carter who had moved into Joanna's vision and was looking towards her in alarm. Joanna shrank away, and as she went her last sight was of that hateful and hating face bit by bit resuming its normal appearance, the last sound that of Delia going off into an hysterical hee-haw.

Hearing her own sobbing breath, Joanna staggered in the dark along the narrow space cleared for her between the properties, her eyes fixed on the yellow oblong which was the outline of the door. She reached it, amazingly, without tripping, and looked out into the corridor.

The corridor was empty of all but a Berkeley girl, realistically repeating the motions of being sick. Or perhaps it was for real. At any rate she was absorbed in her performance and Joanna slipped out of the props room unheeded, sped left, and fell on the door at the end. Sergeant Diggory was on the far side of it and caught her by the shoulders, then let her go when he had looked at her. After that, the narrow twisting corridor was far less of an ordeal. It led eventually to the lobby inside the stage door and Fred's empty booth. There was a policeman at the door, to whom she gasped out her name.

The policeman nodded and Joanna flung out into the night and over to her car. She was mumbling a sort of prayer that it was all being resolved, now, behind her, in the theatre.

"Have you lost Gail?" asked Margaret curiously, in the hall of *Seaview.*

"Gail went on to the theatre." It was a short enough response for her to get it out on one breath and not show she was panting. "Good night."

She smiled as firmly as her tremulous mouth would let her, and went upstairs. She used the bathroom, and when she went back into her bedroom she locked the door and removed the key. There was no need to get out pen and paper because, as Neil had put it, it had shrieked at her. She got into bed and lay down. She heard them come home—car doors slammed and the taxi idled and there was a sharp unhappy laugh. She lay rigid, hoping desperately that unless it was all over no one would come to her room and make her unlock the door. She wanted so much to know what had happened, but she couldn't go out and ask them. She strained her ears as the feet began to pass on the landing.

"I wonder what good *that* did him?" was the only comment she could make out, in Rhoda's voice.

But it was enough to tell her that Neil Carter's experiment had failed, the owner of that wicked face was still at large, under the roof of *Seaview.*

CHAPTER 17

I

In her dream she didn't get across the props room without falling over the baskets and the rails, she stumbled at every step and the oblong of light which was the door and the corridor was always as far away. Once, in the dark, she found herself awake, she thought because she had heard the handle of her door turning. She lay stiff with fear, but perhaps that also was a dream, because the next minute it was day and outside her door were the expected sounds of morning.

By sunlight, although her memory of that face was no less horrible, Joanna was able to tell herself she had only imagined its awareness of her, let alone its awareness of the knowledge which her eyes in the shadows had so briefly betrayed. It was absurd. Nevertheless, she would behave very normally and she would not telephone Neil Carter from the hotel, she would walk into Linton and telephone him from the department store.

She was late going into the dining-room, and they were all assembled. She went straight up to Terry as their leader and asked him, openly and with concern, what had been the outcome of the experiment. She looked round the room as she was speaking and smiled where she caught their eyes. She caught the eyes that had given themselves away the night before, and her smile was returned. That made it easier, at any rate, and her fear even more absurd. Gail had been crying. Terry looked desperately weary. He said:

"Nothing came out of it, unless the Inspector wasn't letting on. I reckon we'll go our ways on Sunday without knowing what happened to Julia, and that no one ever will know. Perhaps it's best."

"Perhaps." She didn't look at those eyes again, just in case, although she was more inclined every moment to think her fear was ridiculous. "I'm sorry you were all—agonised—for nothing."

"Agonised was the word!" shouted Rhoda.

"I'm sorry," muttered Gail.

"Oh, come on!" Rhoda beside her thumped Gail on the shoulder, then put an arm round her. "You couldn't help it."

Joanna had to make an effort to eat any breakfast (and she still felt cautious enough to want to be seen eating), her instinct was to leave while they were all still behind their bacon and eggs and set off for Linton. But she forced herself to take her time, and to wait until some of them had already left the dining-room before strolling out herself. She didn't go upstairs again, she put on a bit more lipstick in the downstairs ladies'.

When she came out there was nobody in the hall except Margaret and she didn't turn to look at the figures she saw in lounge and dining-room out of the corners of her eyes.

She decided to walk into Linton, along the promenade.

2

It was a glorious morning, promise of an Indian summer to come. The sky was paler again and cloudless, the sun warm. Joanna walked steadily, resisting the impulse to look behind her, which would be to admit the possibility of a danger she couldn't really believe in. It seemed a long way.

They brought Neil to the telephone at once. He didn't disguise his relief.

"Oh, Joanna, thank goodness! You're not at *Seaview*, are you?"

She was uneasy.

"No, I'm not. I'm in Arbuthnot's. Neil . . ."

"I just rang *Seaview* and asked for Gail. She inquired discreetly and found you'd gone out."

"Gail . . ."

She realised why she was uneasy. Because Neil was. Neil knew what she had seen. And if Neil knew . . . if she had made it that plain . . . "I *know*, Neil. You know I know. Don't you?"

"I think so."

She said roughly: "Why on earth haven't you done anything about it?"

"Because I haven't got sufficient proof."

"Neil, I don't want to be melodramatic, but . . ."

"I'll pick you up."

"Come here, will you, to Arbuthnot's. I'll meet you in the restaurant."

There was silence.

"Neil?"

"Look," said Neil. "Will you do one more thing for me? Joanna, I swear I won't let it be dangerous. But—I think you could get me my proof. I really think you could."

She said deliberately: "I'm right to be afraid, then?"

"I think so."

She wished he wouldn't keep saying that. It was unaccustomedly mealy-mouthed. But he as well as she must be on unfamiliar territory.

"I *am* afraid, Neil." Her scalp was crawling. "What do you want me to do?"

"I want you," he said slowly, working it out, she thought, as he spoke, "to go to the restaurant at Arbuthnot's and have a coffee. I want you to stay there half an hour—that is"—he paused briefly—"until ten minutes to eleven, and come out through the most open busy parts of the store and walk on up the street and round the corner, up the hill. Stick to the middle of the road until you get to your gap in the wall, then take the plunge through it, and on to the hillside. Synchronise our watches."

She was too tense to be amused by the cliché.

"Then?"

"I'll be there. I'll be there already."

"Neil, I'm sorry, I don't think I can." She was afraid she was going to be sick.

"I'll be able to reach you," said Neil. "Well, you *know* I will, I wouldn't put you in any danger except to your nerves, and those are stronger than appears. Please, Joanna."

The sickness had passed.

"How shall I behave when I get there?"

"When you're through the gap go walking round, breathing deep and stretching your legs. Keep turning round."

"Neil!"

"No, no," he said soothingly, "that's just common sense. You'll be all right, Joanna."

With a sudden thought she looked out over the department in front of her.

"Neil—do you think I'm being watched, now?"

"If we're right, you probably are. No matter. You're obviously trying to get an appointment to see me, which makes—other action—more urgent still."

Yes, to somebody with eyes like those, it would.

Yet she said pleadingly to Neil:

"Perhaps we're wrong. Oh, I don't mean about who killed Julia. I know I'm not wrong about that. But—that I was spotted. Perhaps we're wrong about that."

He said very gently:

"You moved, dear."

3

She had two coffees and two cigarettes. She felt as if a glass wall separated her from the other people in the restaurant. A woman having words with a waitress and stalking out. An ice cream transforming a restless child to an image of absorbed contentment. Two women eagerly talking, two men silent. When someone caught her eye and smiled she smiled back in surprise.

She came out of the restaurant at the precise minute Neil had ordered, descended via the escalators, and left the building by the main door into the main street. As she walked reluctantly, with trembling legs, up towards the bend in the road, she put on her sunglasses. They would take from the dreadful brilliance of those eyes if . . . when . . .

She was round the corner, and was tempted to ask a woman tending a window-box if she might have a glass of water. At least the woman was a cover for her as far as the gap, and it was clear that Neil Carter had wanted her to reach the hillside without incident.

There were sheep, just inside the gap, and they scattered bleating. Joanna moved on, up and over the springy turf, into the vulnerable open. She thought with sudden craven hope that perhaps the trap would be anticipated, and then remembered that the owner of the face she had seen from the props room doorway was not quite sane. To kill Julia, a wildly enormous chance had been taken, and it had paid off. Courage and confidence could only grow—and desperation now discovery was threatened. Neil Carter hadn't shown his knowledge in his eyes. There was a chance that Neil Carter was still in ignorance . . .

Joanna danced about on the hillside, throwing her arms up to the sky as she had done several times in the past weeks before flinging herself down on the turf to dream. It was a sort of a help, being able to express her terror.

She came to a halt facing the gap in the wall, and the small neat figure was just negotiating it, scattering the sheep which had already reassembled. It approached her slowly and steadily, smiling in its usual way which was of course inhuman anyway. It was wearing gloves.

"Hello, Arthur," said Joanna.

He stopped a few feet away from her, and there was absolute silence. Her ears strained vainly into it for a sound from Neil Carter and his men, within saving distance.

Arthur's smile faded and he looked reproachful. He shook his head.

"I'm sorry you got yourself involved, my dear Joanna," he said.

"In what?" she asked shakily. She made no decision to begin by pleading ignorance, it was an instinct of self-preservation.

He shook his head again, smiling more widely. His teeth were very bright. There was no hatred, no passion at all, in his eyes now, just a tranquil certainty.

"I was very clever," said Arthur, "and at one moment only, dear lady, was I taken unawares. Last night." The hatred flickered briefly, dreadfully, across his face, leaving it once more serene. "You are perceptive, my dear, and you took advantage of that moment. In it you learned everything of which Detective Inspector Carter is still in ignorance."

She was so eager she even took a step towards him. "No! No, Arthur, you're wrong there. Neil Carter knows. He knew before last night, so you can be sure that he saw—what I saw." Arthur shook his head. Now there was a tinge of pity in his smile. "That's the truth! And what's more, he's watching us now. He's waiting for his proof, and if—if anything looks like happening to me, he'll be here, and he'll have all the proof he needs."

He shook his head again, and looked round on the peaceful featureless horizon. There was no sound but the anxious bleating of sheep.

"I don't believe you, Joanna. But I do believe that as soon as you do see Neil Carter—and the sooner the better is what you are thinking now—you will make certain that he is not very much longer in ignorance."

"Arthur, for your own sake—believe me." But her voice was weak and unconvincing, even to herself. She was watching fascinated to see what Arthur was drawing out of his pocket.

"For my own sake," he said, "I must protect myself." His hand was out of his pocket now, his gloved hands were embracing, twisting between them what looked like a piece of brown silk. There was nothing limp about Arthur's hands now. But she . . .

Neil Carter was the last detective on earth, if not the last man, to let her down. She tried to see his frowning face in front of her mind's eye, superimpose it on the hideous doll face in front of her.

"Why did you kill Julia?"

The hatred again, making her glad she was behind her sunglasses.

"She said to Geoffrey—to *Geoffrey!*—and to how many others beside . . . she said: 'Arthur's getting past it. Geoffrey, you know this has to be Arthur's last season. We can't support—old duds!' " The face, now, was distorted almost beyond recognition. "Evil, cruel, ignorant woman! To say that of a man who has devoted his life, his talents, his heart . . . Such wicked nonsense." He gave a sob. "But Geoffrey—might have been influenced. And if he wasn't, she would say it again. It was too dangerous. As well as too wanton, too wicked . . ."

She daren't let her attention go, the amount that would be necessary to be sick. Or to faint. Oh, God, she mustn't *faint* . . . "But Arthur, you talk of wickedness! You killed Julia. You took her life away."

"Because she would take away my reason for living. A life for a life, Joanna. Most regrettably, now, a life for two lives."

Arthur's hands were not together, yet the piece of brown silk was still in both of them. It stretched between them, longer and longer as he drew them farther apart. It might have been a stocking. It was nearer to her. Arthur was holding it out, as if offering it to her. There was still silence around them, no beings beyond the silly sheep. There was, after all, nobody near enough to save her, and she would die. It was true that one's past life was briefly, totally, lived again . . .

Joanna cried out, but not because the thread of silk was almost around her throat. She cried out because of the explosion in her head and the clarity which followed it.

She watched in astonishment as Arthur sagged backwards into the arms of two uniformed policemen. His hands flopped to his sides and his short legs folded up underneath him as if he had been a dummy, in the way she had once imagined would happen if Arthur collapsed. As they carried him away he looked pathetically small and limp. There was a flash of white from his slack mouth, and one of the policemen bent hastily over him.

Then Joanna was sick. She straightened up gasping into Neil Carter's arm.

"Litter!" he said accusingly.

"It's organic matter," panted Joanna, "only like apple cores or matches. Oh, Neil!"

"I'll take you back. You were tremendous. We heard you, you know, with our sophisticated devices."

"I want to stay here a bit." The clarity was piercing. It was all round her in the clear bright air. "I want to talk, believe it or not. But don't you have to go?"

"Not yet. Now now." He led her away a little. They sat down on a slight slope and he turned and grinned at her. It was as if a load had gone from him. "Are you sure you're all right? You look a bit done in."

"I've had two shocks. I thought I was going to die."

"I told you I'd be there!" He was almost angry, crushing his fingers into her arm.

"I know, I know. But for a moment—that last moment—I did think it. And as they say—my past life came back to me."

"Yes?" He was looking keenly into her face.

"You knew my husband was dead, Neil."

"Yes."

"That he's been dead more than a year."

"Yes."

"You knew I thought he was alive."

"I knew you couldn't be—pretending, because you went on even when I told you the police had seen your daily and your gardener."

"And you didn't have me locked up or sent to a psychiatrist. Did you think I was ill?"

She had to keep looking round her in her amazement, because of the enormous calm clarity.

"A little. But I knew how he had died. Do you know?"

"Oh, yes. He was killed by a hit-and-run driver in Brussels."

"When exactly did you find out? I mean, remember?"

"In the seconds when that stocking came towards me. When I couldn't run. All that hillside and that little man, but I couldn't run. I thought about so much then. I *saw* the past for the first time since I forgot it. And I still had time to sort of lament that no sooner had I got it back than it was all going to be taken away from me!"

She was able to laugh. Mainly in amazement.

"It was the shock."

"Yes."

He said, again: "I told you I'd be there."

"I know. But there was nothing in the world that I could see except that stocking."

"Years ago," murmured Neil, "he used to give displays in hypnosis."

"Which you didn't tell me."

"In those few moments on the telephone, I honestly forgot. And I didn't think you would run anyway."

They held hands.

"I know so much, Neil, all of a sudden. I feel winded. Perhaps I'll lose it all again if I don't put it into words."

"Yes?"

"I know for instance," she said slowly, "that it wasn't just the shock of Peter's death that sent me off. I don't think I'm *that* weak-minded. It was the guilt—before, and then unbearably afterwards."

"The guilt?"

"You see, I couldn't love him." She had never said it, never, and so she said it again, and louder. A sheep looked inquiringly over the near wall, and this time she found it difficult to stop laughing.

"I lived with him for seventeen years," she said when she had wiped her eyes and blown her nose. "It was a very close marriage, we did everything together. But for me it was going through the motions."

"Did he know?"

"Perhaps he knew more than I did. Because *I* didn't know. I've just put it into words for the first time. All I knew was that for me everything was an effort of the will. The only spontaneous gestures I made towards Peter were gestures of pity because I felt he deserved better. Everything I did with him and for him, I did because I told myself I should. I think I was very hard on myself, every minute of every day. And awake in the night. I thought there must be a defect in my nature, a coldness, and I was sorry for Peter, that this was the kind of woman he had chosen."

"Why on earth did you marry him?"

"He persuaded me it was right. And I think I felt a bit sorry for him even at the start, he meant so well. And—I'd never been in love, I didn't know . . ."

She wasn't looking at him. He said softly:

"Wouldn't you like to go back to *Seaview?*"

"Not yet. We couldn't have children—my fault—and our relationship got more and more claustrophobic and for me less and less real and more and more guilt-making . . ."

"If you could have talked to him . . ."

"But I hadn't even talked to myself. I just felt shabby all the time. Perhaps it wouldn't have been so bad if I hadn't known, somewhere, that I'd made him less than happy. Just before he left for that last time, he said something which I remember now I couldn't get out of my mind, either before he was killed or afterwards. He said: 'At least the love burden is mine. It rarely falls equally, you know. I'm glad I'm carrying it rather than you.'"

"So. He was happy, if he was glad of that."

"Perhaps. And I'm not talking about things as they look now, sitting with my lover high on the hill. I'm talking about how they were down there, when I was imprisoned in them. I always had a pathetic sort of a hope that I would eventually put things right—whatever I meant by that—and then there was no more chance."

"You're not worrying now?"

She looked round her again. "Oh, no. Not now. Or ever again. For better or worse it happened and has come to an end."

"Do you remember about after you heard your husband had been killed?"

"So far and no further. I know I felt more and more guilty and that I took a friend's advice and tried to distract myself with good works. I found I was rather good at them—I couldn't say I enjoyed them because it was so long since I'd enjoyed anything I'd lost the art—but they kept me busy and kept me together. It must have worked—mustn't it?—and then it all disappeared into a fog—and then I was sitting on a chair in the hall at home thinking Peter was still alive in Brussels and realising that I couldn't go on."

"And *Seaview?*"

She told him, now, about *Seaview.*

"I suppose the whole thing was a bit like being under hypnosis." She really thought of Arthur for the first time since they had dragged him away, and started shaking. Neil was tender and coaxing with her, until the shaking stopped. "They say, don't they," she went fluently on, "that you can never be made to do anything under hypnosis you wouldn't do when you were awake, anything against your principles. I've always had what are called high principles—although I wasn't certain even about *that* until just now!—and I must have known somewhere, when I went upstairs with you, Neil, that Peter was dead. I was never unfaithful to him. These last three weeks . . . I'd started to wonder. But I didn't know, I couldn't remember."

She was suddenly tired, and leaned back into his arm.

"You've been very kind. Did you think you would be therapy for me?"

She found she didn't mind if he had thought that, if that was why he had acted as he had. But he didn't respond to the smile she turned to give him. He said gravely:

"No. I just thought—it couldn't be bad."

"It wasn't bad."

She lay back again. She could sleep. She would like to sleep, there and then, against Neil's steady shoulder, hearing nothing but the sheep and their own breathing.

But Neil was helping her to her feet, he was supporting her back to the gap in the wall.

She asked him, as he took his seat beside her in the car: "What will happen to Arthur now?"

"Broadmoor, for a certainty."

"Will you—tell them?"

"Of course."

"I'd still rather not be brought into it."

"Of course not. But can you walk round the corner on your own?"

"If I make up my mind to it."

"Go straight to bed and I'll see that Gail comes up."

Neil dropped her in the side street and she just managed to get home, holding on to the wall here and there.

She passed the dining-room where they had just assembled for lunch, relieved that she would not be there when he told them. She got into bed and lay down. The sleepy languor persisted, and she lay happily wandering about the restored spaces of her mind, looking at the symbols on the walls as if it was a picture gallery. She slid in and out of sleep. At some point Gail came up with a tray, some tablets and a glass of water. She ate everything on the tray and took the tablets, while Gail told her what had gone on in the dining-room. They were sad and shocked and happy, and Gail was no longer set apart.

When Gail had gone Joanna slept more than she woke, and wasn't properly awake until after dark. Then she got out of bed and went to stand at the Window.

The sky was full of stars and there was moonlight far out on the low tide. She was overwhelmed in a sense of thanksgiving. The one thing she had still been afraid of was the past, grimacing here and there through the fog in which she had obscured it. Now she could see it clearly she knew for certain that it was defeated. Knew without a shadow of doubt. For that one calm evening of the aftermath of revelation, there were no shadows at all.

It was a long, rarefied time before it occurred to Joanna how extraordinary it was to have been almost killed by a madman and to esteem it the secondary event of her day. But already the episode which had distracted her was ending and the Murder at the Tivoli would be a very slim volume on the shelves of that great echoing chamber of her life where she was walking and looking and listening.

Only it wasn't finished yet, there was something she still didn't understand and which she wanted to have explained to her. She turned back in a sort of disappointment to the bed, but she knew she would sleep no more without that explanation and she put on her dressing-gown and went rather totteringly downstairs. They must have come back from the theatre while she was unnaturally asleep. She was glad there was nobody about. She went into the telephone booth and dialled *The Feathers Hotel.* While she waited to be put through the necessity of the explanation grew more and more urgent, as the desire to see a film grows when one finds one has to queue. She didn't even care that she would probably be waking Neil from a hard-earned sleep. Anyway, there was a telephone by his bed.

"What are you doing out of bed?" he greeted her crossly.

"I'll go straight back. But I couldn't sleep without speaking to you first."

"Oh no?"

She saw his salesman's smile in her mind's eye, but that was unfair, it was so rarely now she saw it in fact. Perhaps she didn't want to think that he might be wearing a quite different expression.

"Oh, that as well," she answered, with a flirtatious indifference she had never used, or had any instinct for, in the days before the fog. Where had she been during her absence? Or perhaps she should ask, what hidden parts of herself were coming through? It was a subject for study during the solitude ahead. "But what I wanted to ask you about was Pam. I seem destined one way and another to forget Pam. Was she the lead?"

"She was. What nerve that girl has got! She overheard the conversation between Geoffrey and Julia which Arthur overheard. He was in the corridor just outside the open dressing-room door and she was in the famous props room. She saw him, and saw his face. I don't have to describe the set-up."

"No."

"He didn't see her, *bien entendu.* But she was shaken, and when Julia was killed a few days later, she was terrified. She tried to feel better by thinking she was being silly, imagining what she'd seen, and it worked for a while. But then . . ."

"She couldn't think she'd imagined that, Neil."

"No."

"And all the time she went on quietly smiling."

"Nerve, as I said. Plus a certain amount of what you and I would call insensitivity."

"And she withdrew into kiddology again."

"I think, into just not wanting to be involved. Such a self-preservative instinct can go to enormous lengths—or should I say *not* go to them—as you'll have read frequently in the papers."

"Yes. Didn't Geoffrey tell you about the conversation, about what Julia thought of Arthur?"

"Not until I told him Pam's version of it! Oh, he just forgot. After I'd broken Pam down I went to Scarborough and confronted Geoffrey and he apologetically corroborated. He hadn't of course known that Arthur was listening, or Pam either. But I could have killed him. If he'd told me at once I'd at least have had an idea where to look, and not spent most of my sweat in the wrong directions. And it was Geoffrey who gave me a dissertation on the old vocational comedians!"

"Poor Neil."

"It's amazing, really. Julia juggled all those men, with a grotesque sort of skill, and then signed her death warrant with a chance remark that really didn't have anything to do with her own dangerous life."

"Another thing, too. It's such a small part of it all that's really been solved. The Berkeley girls still hate their mother, and Vincent's still in a dither, and Gail's still in love with Terry, and . . ."

"And we're getting philosophical. I was going to phone you in the morning. Will you come to *The Feathers* for lunch on Sunday?"

"I'd love it. But I'm surprised you'll still be around."

"Just. Not because I have to be."

"Thank you, Neil."

"Go back to bed."

Hall and landing were still deserted. She pictured them each in their rooms, absorbing Neil's revelation. She was after all still very much concerned with them. Already, the loftiness of her own revelation had passed into memory.

CHAPTER 18

I

When Joanna woke up on Saturday morning she decided she would like to have breakfast in bed, and for the first time since her arrival at *Seaview* she rang the bell. Margaret came in so quickly Joanna suspected her of hovering on the landing. It was half past nine. Joanna stayed in bed until eleven, reading her paper from cover to cover and feeling pleasantly convalescent.

When she got downstairs there were already a few large cases in the hall. Dirk and Delia were superintending the removal of two of them, into the hands of a man in the uniform of British Rail whose yellow van stood at the gate. Mrs. Tompkins was in evidence, effusing slightly. Miss Waterhouse, glimpsed in the recesses of the office, looked more weary and distracted than ever.

It was as if everything was already over and done with, and there was only the tidying up.

Joanna went out and started to walk into town along the beach, trying not to think of her first walk into Linton, when she had hurried after Terry Dawson. But she saw him again ahead of her, walking alone with bent head and hands behind his back. This time she was careful not to let the distance narrow between them. Eventually she stopped and sat down on the sand because she had begun to cry. She sat there for a long time, hugging her knees and crying and calling it reaction. When she stopped she got up and went on into town and round Marks and Spencer's, where she bought a few practical and unexciting things.

At lunch she realised how much tension there had been, because it had gone. She saw the truth of Gail's pronouncement that the jokes and the laughter and the occasional knockabout had been ritualistic, because now they were spontaneous. Regret sharpened in her and she watched it warily, because it must not threaten the next phase of her life which would begin tomorrow. To escape it, at least to keep it under control, she drove a few miles away from Linton in the afternoon. Inland, but not towards Wincaster. She took Gail with her, and they had an early tea in the garden of a country inn. Gail seemed restored, beautiful, confident, looking towards a holiday in Spain and then rehearsals for pantomime.

More things could now be said.

"Have you got a boyfriend, Gail?"

"Oh, Bruce," she said indifferently, "but he's easy enough to go on holiday with, and he makes sure everything runs all right."

"D'you feel better now about Terry?"

She had said it before she remembered that Gail's love for Terry was something they had never directly spoken of, but she didn't draw back.

"No." Gail didn't seem surprised at the question. She looked down at her plate, kneading cake crumbs. "I don't, but that's nothing to do with Terry. I've just got to get over it." She shook her head over the plate. "I thought at one time perhaps you . . ." she said eventually.

"Oh, no!" Gail's head jerked up, because Joanna was so vehement. "Oh, no," said Joanna again, more quietly, "we just liked one another." That was the one mystery which would never be solved, why Terry had ceased to like her.

"Anyway, you've got a husband," said Gail smiling, tilting her chin, making an effort to go full speed ahead.

"I haven't actually."

She told Gail a bit about what had happened to her, before and after the stocking in Arthur's hands. It was beautiful in the garden of the inn, they sat at the edge of a lawn enclosed by old walls, blackbirds were splashing in the grey stone bird bath. But Gail would be late for first house if they didn't leave in a hurry.

Gail kept laughing on the way back, at the thought of being late for the first time on the last evening.

When they got to *Seaview* Joanna went upstairs and sat in the Window and wrote indifferently to Daphne to tell her she would be coming home only in order to sell up. Then she wrote to the relevant soul in each of the organisations she belonged to, resigning.

2

She was in the same seat at the Tivoli. The audience were buzzing with an extra excitement, because of the screaming felt-pen letters on the billboard at the theatre doors, where they sold the local evening paper. A few of the older women were in tears. Joanna even saw a pair of arms go out towards the stage as the curtain rose and the players were revealed smiling bravely in the golden light.

But the response of the whole audience was tremendous, a surge of love and longing towards the stage. Joanna hoped at first that her own fierce response was merely a reaction to the general mood, but by the interval it had begun to alarm her and she went out to the café in the hope that by stretching her legs, drinking coffee, doing something, she could get it under control.

She was there so quickly she was served at once, and she sat down with her coffee in a corner. She felt more alarmed still when she saw Terry, his pink and gold half hidden by a velvet jacket, moving round the café and shaking people's hands, having his head pulled down by an imperious female arm for a kiss, signing books. At first she tried not to look at him, darting so rapidly but so gently about the room, but in the end she watched him avidly, moving her head so that she could still see him when he went behind people or pillars, and when he came by her table she put out her hand and took hold of his arm. She said despairingly:

"Terry . . ."

He hadn't noticed her, and she felt his arm jerk under her hand. His public expression slipped away as he looked at her, and then she was shocked, at his bleak haggard face. He stared grimly at her, not moving out of the tense circle of her fingers.

"Go home to your husband, Joanna," he said at last. "Go home to him!"

"Terry!"

He had moved on, but she had let her hand fall from his arm at the impact of the joy. She got up and began to walk back towards the auditorium. It was only now the pain had gone that she realised how bad it had been.

She bumped against Neil Carter in the doorway of the café, and looked at him in dazed surprise. He took her arm.

"I'm glad I've found you," he said. He walked her into the theatre and they sat down on two seats at the end of the nearest row.

"I didn't think you were coming to the show tonight." It was like an encounter in a dream.

"I wasn't. I haven't. I came to catch *you.* Joanna, I'm so sorry—for myself, I mean—but I can't have lunch with you after all tomorrow, I've got to get back to London tonight. Chief's orders, something has broken."

"Oh, I'm sorry too, Neil. I was looking forward to it."

There was a pause. She didn't have either the will or the energy to initiate more conversation.

"You're not going back home, are you?" asked Neil.

"Only to sell up. Oh, no, I couldn't go back there." She was aware of him looking at her all the time, but she could only give him brief glances.

"Are you going to stay at *Seaview,* then?"

"Well, for a while, yes. Oh, yes, I'll stay at *Seaview.*"

"I can get in touch with you there, then."

"Oh, yes." She made an effort. "Of course, Neil."

He had been looking in his wallet, and held out his card to her.

"That has both my home and office details. You should come to London, you know. It would be good for you, and we could see each other—more regularly than if you stay down here. It would be fun."

Oh, yes, it would. In a flash, she saw a succession of scenes: dining well at different places, lying in the grass of a park, seeing an exhibition, a play, caring for each other's opinions, being sharp with each other before being gentle, always alive and alert. If only . . .

As she at last looked him full in the face she felt the rejection in her eyes. There were a few seconds of silence.

"But on the other hand," said Neil, "as I'm not the long-term type and I think you are . . ."

She wasn't in a dream, she was awake and feeling, more immediately than her happiness, regretful and sad. She had perhaps just thrown something of value away. She would never know for certain whether Neil had always intended to caution her, or whether he had done it to defend himself against her, to get out first. But she thought she knew.

She clutched after the card he was withdrawing, secured it, and put it into her bag.

"I won't come to London without contacting you," she said, trying to sound cheerful, "accepting what you've just said."

He got up and she saw that the people whose places they had taken were wanting to sit down. She followed him into the aisle. The worst thing she could do to Neil Carter—either the cruellest or the most misplaced—would be to try and make up for anything. She said, "Well, goodbye," kissed his cheek, and turned away. She wanted dreadfully to turn back, to go back, to tell him how special he was, but she kept on, into her seat, and he didn't follow her.

She was a battleground for a while, but the show was insistent, and most of the time Terry was on stage.

Without deciding to do it she crept out of her seat during the noisy finale and went through the dividing door, and when Terry was singing alone on the dark stage she was standing in the wings. She would wait there, catch him as he came off, she would wait despite being in everybody's way. But as the curtain fell she found herself running on to the stage, up to Terry as he got to his feet.

"Terry, I'm a widow. I didn't know. I'm a widow, Terry, I'm free!"

The lights went up on his astonished face. They blinked at one another. And then that sweet gentle smile, the smile he gave only to those he loved, his audience.

"We'll go home tonight," said Terry, "on our own. I reckon we could do with a chat."

Her joy almost choked her.

"Terry . . ."

"For heaven's sake," said Terry, "get off the stage."

Only then she noticed the cast were coming back. Terry pulled her into the wings, squeezing between the last of the oncoming players. She had her back to the wall, he had a hand each side of her.

"Being the last night," he said, "there'll be speeches and flowers. You'll have to wait."

"I'll wait."

He bent forward and kissed her before going back on stage to lead *The Queen.*

Eileen Dewhurst was born in Liverpool and educated there at Huyton College, and later at Oxford. As a free-lance journalist, she has published many articles in the *Liverpool Daily Post,* the *Illustrated Liverpool News, Punch,* and *The Times.* She has written plays which have been performed in England, and is the author of four other crime novels, two of which–*Trio in Three Flats* and *Drink This*–have been published by the Crime Club.

Fic. 1982 81-3290

PR 6054 .E95 C8 1982

Dewhurst, Eileen.

Curtain fall